The Paradise Affair

Carpenter and Quincannon Mysteries

The Paradise Affair

A CARPENTER AND QUINCANNON MYSTERY

BILL PRONZINI

A TOM DOHERTY ASSOCIATES BOOK NEW YORK

THE PARADISE AFFAIR

Copyright © 2020 by Pronzini-Muller Family Trust

A Forge Book
Published by Tom Doherty Associates
120 Broadway
New York, NY 10271

www.tor-forge.com

Forge® is a registered trademark of Macmillan Publishing Group, LLC.

The Library of Congress Cataloging-in-Publication Data is available upon request.

ISBN 978-1-250-21650-2 (hardcover)
ISBN 978-1-250-21651-9 (ebook)

Our books may be purchased in bulk for promotional, educational, or business use. Please contact your local bookseller or the Macmillan Corporate and Premium Sales Department at 1-800-221-7945, extension 5442, or by email at MacmillanSpecialMarkets@macmillan.com.

First Edition: January 2021

Printed in the United States of America

0 9 8 7 6 5 4 3 2 1

For Marcia

The Paradise Affair

1

QUINCANNON

The one thing above all others that Quincannon could not abide was failure.

Failure was an affront to his pride and his skills as a detective, a threat to his mental health if not his very career. It infuriated and frustrated him. It plunged him into a morass of gloom, nagging and rankling after the fashion of an infected tooth.

A long time had passed since he'd last tasted the bitterness of defeat. He hadn't expected he would ever taste it again. Now, faced with the evident fact that his infuriatingly elusive quarry had permanently escaped his clutches, it was as if his mouth had been stuffed with ashes. Two weeks of intense investigative work, all for nothing!

He glowered at the Matson Navigation Company clerk, a look of such ferocity that the man paled; the business card Quincannon had given him dropped to the counter as if it had suddenly burned his fingers. "You're certain those two men embarked for the Hawaiian Islands on Saturday?"

"Yes, sir. Their names are on the *Roderick Dhu*'s passenger list. James A. Varner and Simon Reno."

Those were aliases, not their true names, but that was none of the clerk's business. "Did they actually depart?" Quincannon demanded. "You know that for a fact?"

"They must have, sir, or their names would not be on the list. They each booked a first-class cabin."

"To Honolulu, not to Australia or someplace in the Far East? You're sure of that, too?"

"Yes, sir. Honolulu is their final destination."

"One-way or round-trip tickets?"

"Round-trip."

"Date of return passage also booked?"

"No, sir. Round-trip tickets are valid for three months, so passengers often delay booking their return voyage."

Hell, damn, and blast! "Did you personally sell them the tickets?"

"Yes, sir," the clerk said. "Friday afternoon, the day before the *Roderick Dhu* sailed. I remember them because they each paid the one-hundred-and-fifty-dollar fee in gold specie."

"Describe them."

The clerk did so. One tall, dark, slender, well dressed, the possessor of a mane of silvery hair; the other short, stout, red-haired, also well dressed, and sporting an imperial beard. Unquestionably the two birds Quincannon had been chasing. Incredible as it seemed, they had not only managed to fly away, they had flown the blasted country.

"May I ask why you're looking for these men, sir?"

Quincannon said, "No, you may not," turned on his heel, and stomped out into the cold, wet, early-May morning. Another dreary day in a string of dreary days, a perfect match for his mood.

Hoolihan's Saloon was marginally closer to the Matson Navigation Company's office than to the Market Street base of Carpenter and Quincannon, Professional Detective Services. He went there first because it was a familiar place of refuge, and because he was not yet ready to face Sabina with the news of his failure.

The Second Street resort had been his favorite in his drinking days. It was there that he had sought for two long years to drown his guilty conscience after the incident in Virginia City, Nevada, when a young woman named Katherine Bennett, eight months pregnant, had perished with a bullet from his pistol in her breast. The shooting, a tragic accident, had happened during a gun battle that erupted when he and a team of local law enforcement officers attempted to arrest a pair of brothers who were counterfeiting U.S. government currency. In the skirmish one of the brothers wounded a deputy and then fled through the backyards of a row of nearby houses. Quincannon had shot the man, to avoid being shot himself; but one of his bullets had ricocheted wildly and found Katherine Bennett, who had been outside hanging up her washing.

That had been the darkest day of his life by far. The burden of responsibility for the loss of two innocent lives had been unbearable; guilt and remorse had eaten away at him, led him to take so heavily to drink that he'd been in danger of losing his position as a Secret Service operative. Two things saved him: the first was another counterfeiting case that led him to the Owyhee Mountains of Idaho; the second was meeting Sabina, then a "Pink Rose" attached to the Pinkerton Agency's Denver office, who was there on an undercover assignment of her own. Their investigations had combined, and the successful resolutions to both had led him to make peace with himself and to the eventual creation of their detective partnership. Not a drop of alcohol had passed his lips since then, nor ever would again.

Nevertheless, he continued to frequent Hoolihan's on a sporadic basis, or had until he and Sabina tied the marital knot six months ago. His visit there today was only his second in that half year's time. He had always felt comfortable among its clientele of small merchants, office workers, tradesmen, drummers, and less rowdy waterfront habitués. It was dark and bare in comparison to the uptown, Cocktail Route saloons, illuminated as it was by old-style gaslights. Sawdust was spread thick on the floor, and there were back-room pool and billiard tables on which Quincannon had often honed his considerable skills with a cue.

The other lure for him in the old days had been Hoolihan's free lunch, the best free lunch in the city in his estimation—corned beef, strong cheese, rye bread, bowls of hard-boiled eggs and tubs of briny pickles. But he had no appetite for any of the fare today. Nor any desire to trade the usual good-natured and mildly profane insults with Ben Joyce, the head barman. He ordered his usual tipple, a mug of steaming clam juice, and sat at a corner table letting it warm his hands and his insides while he reflected gloomily on what he'd been told by the Matson Company clerk.

James A. Varner and Simon Reno. Two of the many fictitious names utilized by the slick and slippery grifters he had pursued the past two weeks, and who had escaped his clutches by inexplicably sailing away to what had formerly been known as the Sandwich Islands. Their true names: Jackson "Lonesome Jack" Vereen—the "Lonesome Jack" an ironical moniker, for he was a libertine of gargantuan appetites—and E. B. Nagle, better known as Nevada Ned, whose primary vice was the opium derivative morphine.

During their lengthy careers, the pair had first engaged in bait-and-switch and gold-brick trickery, then graduated to confidence games involving phony stock swindles that netted greater profits. They had been arrested half a dozen times in three states and tried once for their crimes (case dismissed for insufficient evidence), and had yet to serve a single day in prison. Their latest mark had been R. W. Anderson, a *nouveau riche* Oakland resident who owned several East Bay dry goods establishments and who had recently begun investing in the stock market. Vereen and Nagle had made his acquaintance and insinuated themselves into his confidence by posing as Eastern investors with inside knowledge of the commodities market.

Mr. Anderson had allowed himself to be talked into the purchase of two thousand dollars' worth of bogus shares in a nonexistent Nevada silver mine. This error in judgment had been exacerbated by the commission of a mistake even more egregious: Anderson, a trusting soul, had permitted the two swindlers to examine his slim but valuable portfolio of stock certificates and bearer bonds, then foolishly left them alone in his private office while he went to answer a call of nature. The two miscreants, naturally, had seized the opportunity to make off with the portfolio.

Embarrassment, distrust of the police, fear that word would get out and damage his standing in the community had kept him from reporting the theft. It had taken all his courage to seek the aid of a private agency, he admitted to Quincannon—that, plus a healthy dose of anger, a burning desire to see the thieves punished, and the slim hope that the stock certificates and bearer bonds could be recovered. He had chosen Carpenter and Quincannon, Professional Detective Services, because of the agency's reputation for discretion as well as success.

Anderson was willing to pay handsomely for their services, but this was not the only factor in the decision to undertake a full-time investigation on his behalf. Quincannon didn't often feel sorry for his clients, but he felt sorry for this one—a pleasant, well-meaning, harmless gent who had been badly used and who was suffering miserably as a result.

His mouth quirked sardonically. He felt even sorrier for Mr. Anderson now. Yes, and not a little for himself.

He had been confident—overconfident, as much as he hated to admit it—that nabbing Vereen and Nagle would prove to be neither a difficult nor a lengthy undertaking. For one thing, he had had no trouble identifying them from Anderson's descriptions and the agency's file of dossiers of known confidence men. And for another they were known habitués of the more sordid fleshpots when financially solvent.

He had tracked them through known and newly uncovered associates, both female and male, from the East Bay to San Francisco, then south to San Jose, where the pair had succeeded in cashing one of the bearer bonds, then back again to San Francisco. Twice he had come near to closing in on them, only to be foiled by cussed misfortune. He had been sure he was close to nabbing them when he learned that they had been seen in Charles Riley's high-toned Polk Street gamblers' mecca, House of Chance, and that one of the waiters there overheard them planning to make the rounds of the Uptown Tenderloin parlor houses. That usually meant not one but several nights of debauchery, which made it likely that they could still be found in the district.

But this turned out not to be the case. The pair had sampled the exotic wares in three establishments—Miss Bessie Hall's notorious O'Farrell Street establishment, Lettie Carew's Fiddle Dee Dee, and Madame Lucy's Ye Olde Whore Shoppe. But Madame Lucy's had been their last stop. And it was there that the trail ended. A painted and powdered, red-haired nymphet informed Quincannon, upon receipt of a gold sovereign, that after having been serviced by her, Lonesome Jack had drunkenly boasted that he and his partner were soon to embark on a voyage to the "Crossroads of the Pacific."

Quincannon hadn't believed it. A false boast, surely, one of Vereen's habitual fabrications. The pair's bases of operations ranged from Seattle to Los Angeles and points inland; never once had they traveled so far as Mexico, much less to a far-flung island in the Pacific Ocean. Yet he had no other leads, so this morning he had begun canvassing the shipping companies that offered passenger service to various ports in the South Pacific. And now, after his interview with the Matson clerk, there could be no doubt that the pair were in fact bound for Honolulu, Hawaii.

Why, blast it? A lark? Unlikely, given their past history. It must be that they had stumbled onto a new mark and were plotting a swindle as profitable as, if not more so than, the one they had perpetrated on R. W. Anderson. The red-haired bawd had had no knowledge of who or what the new game might involve, nor had Quincannon picked up so much as a whisper or a hint at any time during his search.

And what of the stock certificates and the rest of the bearer bonds? Had Vereen and Nagle taken those with them, or had they stashed them somewhere in the city? In either case he saw no way of finding out, no way of recovering the documents or the two thousand dollars in cash.

The clot of unanswerable questions made the galling taste of failure that much more bitter.

2

QUINCANNON

Sabina was at her desk, engaged in the writing of a report or perhaps a letter, when he entered the offices of Carpenter and Quincannon, Professional Detective Services. He had spent regrettably little time with her the past two weeks; being with her now should serve to lift his spirits, relieve his dour mood, but he suspected that it wouldn't.

He answered her smile with a weak one of his own, then shed his rain-spotted Chesterfield and derby and hung them on the coat tree. Seated at his desk, he loaded his briar from the pouch of Navy Cut. Sabina had gifted him with a flint cigar and pipe lighter at Christmas, and while he preferred matches, he had to admit that the lighter was an improvement over sulfur-smelling lucifers. Or it was when it worked properly. Which it chose not to do this morning. He muttered, "Confounded thing!," fished in his desk for a match, and commenced a furious puffing to get the tobacco burning evenly.

Sabina had replaced her pen in its holder and was watching him quizzically. "What's the matter, John? Why are you so glum?"

He hadn't told her what he'd learned from the Tenderloin bawd last night, believing as he had that it was probably a falsehood. And he'd left the Leavenworth Street flat alone early this morning, instead of sharing the trolley ride to Market Street with her as he usually did, in order to canvass the shipping companies that offered passenger service to the Hawaiian Islands. So she had had no foreknowledge of the calamity that had struck him.

"Lonesome Jack Vereen and Nevada Ned Nagle." Speaking the two names left a bitter taste like that of camphor.

"What about them? What happened?"

"Nothing happened, curse the luck," Quincannon said. "They're gone. Long gone. Far gone."

"Far gone? You mean they've left California?"

"Not only California—the United States. They're on their merry way to Honolulu."

"Honolulu! Are you serious?"

"Never more," he said bleakly. "Departed on a Matson steamship on Saturday."

"Hawaii, of all places. Why, for heaven's sake?"

"Not for a vacation from crime, that's bloody certain. Otherwise I've not a clue."

Sabina folded her hands together on the desktop. "Tell me what you do know and how you found it out."

He told her, puffing out great clouds of bluish smoke as he did so.

"You mustn't blame yourself, John," she said when he finished. Sympathetic, but also practical as was her wont. "You had no way of knowing those rogues were planning a trip to Hawaii."

"No, but I should have caught up to them in time to prevent them from leaving. I had two blasted weeks."

"Not every investigation plays out quickly, you know that."

"That doesn't make their escape or the loss of our client's property any easier to accept."

"Do you suppose they took the bonds and stock certificates with them?"

"At a guess I'd say yes. But I have no way of knowing, and it hardly matters now."

"Perhaps it does," she said. "What do you intend to do?"

"Do? What can I do?"

"You could go after them."

". . . All the way to Honolulu? That is hardly feasible."

"Why isn't it feasible?"

Quincannon pawed his left ear, the lobe of which had been removed by a would-be assassin's bullet the previous year. Sabina insisted its loss had not disfigured him, but he couldn't seem to break himself of the habit of fingering the scar tissue in moments of stress.

"For more than one good reason," he said. "Travel time to Honolulu is seven days, so I was told, and passenger vessels depart only on weekends; by the time I arrived they would have been there a full week. Trying to find them would be prohibitively difficult."

"Not necessarily. Most of the population is native Hawaiian and Chinese, and there are relatively few Caucasian visitors."

"How do you know that?"

"I read newspaper articles, among other things, that don't engage your interest," Sabina said. "The point is a pair of newcomers with profligate ways surely wouldn't escape notice."

"Upon arrival, perhaps not," Quincannon admitted. "But if they have a game on, their pattern has been to put a hold on public indulgence of their vices so as not to call attention to themselves. For all I know a week is enough time for them to finish their scurvy business, whatever it is, and be ready for a return voyage."

"It's just as likely they will be in the midst of it. The high-profit swindles they specialize in take time to set up."

"Yes, but where and with whom? The game doesn't have to be in Honolulu or even on Oahu. There are three or four other islands—"

"Eight altogether in the Hawaiian archipelago."

"Eight makes the odds that much longer."

"Well, you could seek the aid of the police."

"In a backwater foreign country? They're bound to be as inept as the bluecoats here."

"Hawaii is not a foreign country," Sabina reminded him. "The Sandwich Islands Kingdom was overthrown and Queen

Lili'uokalani's reign ended in January of '93, five years ago. If President McKinley and his partisans have their way, the Republic of Hawaii will be annexed as a United States territory later this year."

"And if Japan doesn't invade and annex it first, as they have threatened to do."

"That isn't likely to happen. It was last year that the Japanese dispatched warships, and only for a short time. The threat hasn't materialized."

Quincannon said gloomily, "It still might if this ill-advised war with Spain drags on."

"The belief in Washington is that the war will end quickly. It has been only three weeks since the president signed the congressional resolution authorizing use of force to drive the Spanish out of Cuba."

"War with Spain over the independence of a Caribbean island, and all because of a naval ship that may not have been sunk by sabotage as claimed. 'Remember the *Maine*!' Bah."

"If not a consultation with the police," Sabina said doggedly, "then why not engage the services of a member of our profession? Honolulu is a city of some size; there must be at least one private investigative agency. The Pinkertons would know."

Quincannon gave his mutilated ear another tug. "Do you know what a round-trip ticket to Honolulu costs? The confiscatory sum of one hundred and fifty dollars. On top of which add the price of lodging, transportation rentals, and an added professional fee among other expenses. No, my dear, it just won't do. Our client would never sanction such a trip."

"He might given the circumstances," Sabina said. "R. W. Anderson is a wealthy and an angry man, as you well know. The return of some or all of his stocks and bonds and the ruin of those two thieves is vital to him. You've had his financial support for two weeks now. Would you consider making the trip if he agreed to finance it?"

"Why are you so keen on the prospect of my going?" he said. "If I didn't know better I might think you want to be rid of me."

"Stuff and nonsense. I'm only thinking of your welfare. I know how you hate to mark an investigation unresolved and I couldn't bear to see you mired in the doldrums for the Lord knows how long . . ."

Abruptly Sabina grew silent, her expression becoming oddly introspective. His gaze lingered on her; she was never more attractive to him than when she was in repose. On another day, in a better frame of mind, he would have been content to sit and admire her fine cameo features, her bright blue eyes and raven-black hair, her engaging smile, and count himself the luckiest of men to have her as his bride of six months. But not on this day. After a time her silence, broken only by the pattering of raindrops on the office roof and windows, became a trifle bemusing.

Quincannon tapped the bowl of his briar on the desktop to break her reverie. When he had her attention he asked, "What is it you're thinking so hard about?"

"An idea, John. A rather wonderful idea."

"Yes? And that is?"

"Why don't we both travel to Honolulu?"

Quincannon's whiskers bristled like those on a startled dog. He stared at her. "Surely you're joking."

"Not at all. Despite the war, there have been no warnings against travel to the Islands. There is no real danger to the citizenry or to visitors; the troops being sent to protect Pearl Harbor will see to that. We have no pressing business on the docket other than the Anderson investigation, and I can help you track down Vereen and Nagle—"

"Anderson would never agree to paying passage for both of us."

"No, nor should he be asked to," Sabina said. "Our bank balance is substantial, as you well know. We can certainly afford to pay for my passage and expenses."

He had a brief vision of hard-earned greenbacks vanishing in puffs of smoke. "And what would you do when your assistance was not needed?"

"The same things you can do once the swindlers have been found," Sabina said. "Explore Honolulu and Oahu, sample exotic foods, lounge on a bathing beach . . . become indolent lotus-eaters for a change. The weather is *warm* in the Islands, John, not cold and dreary as it has been and may well continue to be here."

"No," he said, "it's a daft notion."

"Daft? Why is it daft?"

"Fourteen days at sea round trip. Another week or more on the hunt, and with no guarantee of success. Think of the business we'd lose if we closed the agency for three weeks to a month."

"Chances are we wouldn't lose much at all. And we would not have to close the agency. I'm sure Elizabeth Petrie would be willing to take temporary charge, as she has in the past when we've both been away, and she and our part-time operatives could handle most new investigations or their preliminaries." Then, after a pause, she said pointedly, "Besides, your undercover job at the Monarch Mine last fall might well have lasted a month and you had no qualms about accepting that. Or have you forgotten?"

"I haven't forgotten," Quincannon said. "But that was a lucrative business decision, and the assignment was completed in less than three weeks."

"It still meant a postponement of our wedding."

"I've apologized for that any number of times, my dear. But it has nothing to do with this fanciful notion of yours—"

"Fanciful? We have done nothing but labor long hours since November, and we have been apart far too much of the time. We deserve a vacation, even if it is a working one. Yes, and a second honeymoon, too."

"What was wrong with our first honeymoon?"

"Not a thing," she said. "It was lovely. But you must admit it was also quite brief, and the Valley of the Moon a place we had been to before. A pair of seven-day ocean voyages and a week on a tropical island would be a unique and memorable experience, one that would do us both a world of good."

Quincannon said stubbornly, "No, it's out of the question."

"Not even if Mr. Anderson should agree to pay your passage?"

"Not in any case."

"Is that your final word?"

"It is. Neither of us is going to Hawaii."

His final word? Hah. He should have known better.

It took Sabina less than a day to change his mind.

She did not resort to pleading or cajoling to have her way; her woman's wiles were too finely honed for that sort of ploy. Subtlety and finesse were her weapons. Without informing him beforehand, she sent a wire to R. W. Anderson and received by return wire confirmation of the investor's willingness to finance his portion of an Island trip. She consulted with the local Pinkerton office and obtained the name of a reputable Honolulu private investigator, a former police constable named George Fenner. She also obtained Elizabeth Petrie's promise to take charge of the agency in the event of their absence.

Thus armed, Sabina then commenced a forceful promotional campaign. If he didn't seize the opportunity to close out his pursuit of Lonesome Jack Vereen and Nevada Ned and maintain his unblemished record, he would never forgive himself. He was, after all, the most accomplished detective in the western United States. Hadn't he said more than once that he prided himself on never giving up on an investigation when there was so much as a remote chance of success?

Once this baited hook was firmly set, she dwelt on the virtues of ocean travel by steamship—first-class accommodations, sumptuous cuisine, a restful atmosphere conducive to passionate interludes.

And, bolstered by a pamphlet she had found somewhere, she enumerated the virtues of the Hawaiian Islands and Honolulu, Crossroads of the Pacific. Lauded by such luminaries as Robert Louis Stevenson and Mark Twain, who called them "the loveliest fleet of islands anchored in any ocean," they were a virtual paradise where lush vegetation grew in aromatic profusion, the sky was a soft blue, balmy trade winds wafted gently over white sand beaches, sunbrowned Polynesian girls performed native dances clad in little more than grass skirts and flower *leis*. Could he justify denying himself the pleasure of a once-in-a-lifetime experience? Could he justify denying her that same pleasure merely because it would cost a few hundred dollars they could easily afford?

No, he couldn't. And so he weakened and gave in. And not as reluctantly as he might have, after due consideration.

Both of them were going to Hawaii.

3

SABINA

They sailed Saturday noon on the Oceanic steamship *Alameda*.

Sabina had taken care of most of the necessary preparations. She bought their tickets at the company's office on Market Street, having chosen passage on the *Alameda* over one of the Matson Company steamers because of its size—it was a relatively new three-thousand-ton iron ship with accommodations for one hundred first-class, second-class, and steerage passengers. She withdrew from the agency's account at the Miner's Bank what she judged to be enough cash to last them for the duration—more than ever-thrifty John would have taken if she'd left the task up to him. She obtained and packed steamer and wardrobe trunks with appropriate lightweight summer clothing, then arranged to have them transported to the Oceanic Steamship Company wharf at the foot of Steuart and Folsom streets. She spent half a day preparing Elizabeth Petrie, the highly competent former police matron, for her duties during their temporary absence. She also notified her erstwhile cousin Callie French (who was delighted at the news) and a handful of other close friends of their plans.

John, meanwhile, did little other than inform their half-dozen major clients and Whit Slattery and two other part-time male employees. But she didn't mind. She was, after all, more organized and detail-oriented than he, and more excited at the prospect of the trip. Not that he lacked enthusiasm—once committed, he allowed as how he was looking forward to it. Of course that was because of the opportunity to close out the Anderson case; he didn't share her absorption in the voyage and the mystique of the Hawaiian Islands. But he would once they were under way and if his quest for the two swindlers went as well as she hoped it would after their arrival.

The morning was overcast but dry when she and John arrived at the Oceanic wharf shortly before eleven o'clock—a good omen after more than a week of rain, drizzle, and thick fog. Freight wagons, baggage vans, hansom cabs, and other passenger equipage packed the wharfside. Stevedores and winch operators outnumbered arriving passengers by five to one, busily loading all sorts of crates, boxes, sacks, and drums onto the cargo decks; like all the other ships on the Hawaii and Far East runs, the *Alameda* was mainly a transporter of mail and essential trade goods. A scattering of porters trundled passenger baggage up an aft gangplank, while passengers boarded on a forward one. A babel of voices joined with the squeal of winches and the deep-throated bellows of bay foghorns to create a constant din.

Once they alighted from the cab, John took her arm and steered her through the mass of humanity to the forward gangplank. She fancied that they made a particularly attractive couple, John in his Chesterfield, pearl-gray suit, and Panama hat, she in a hooded green and white wool cape and a traveling bonnet trimmed with crushed silk ribbons. He was a ruggedly handsome man, John Frederick— broad shoulders, piercing brown eyes, his full beard neatly trimmed at her insistence. A fine catch, as more than one of her women friends had said to her. And a good husband in every way; the past six months had exceeded her marital expectations. Their future together was bright—if only he would learn to be less reckless in his investigative pursuits. Stephen had made her a widow by engaging in a rash confrontation with bandits near Denver; she could not bear to lose John, too, to an act of violence. . . .

She put that morbid thought out of her head as they boarded the steamer. Days of restful pleasure lay ahead—a grand adventure no matter what the outcome of the search for the two grifters. She was determined that they both enjoy it to the fullest.

A steward directed them to their cabin on A deck amidships. It was spacious and well appointed, as comfortable as a room in a fashionable hotel. It had electric lights, fan, and bell signals to their steward's quarters, as well as easy access to several bathrooms. The steamer's other first-class passenger attractions—dining saloon, music room, library and reading room, smoking rooms and ladies' lounge—were also on this deck.

Rather than remain in the cabin prior to sailing, they went out on deck to stand at the railing with a handful of other passengers willing to brave the cold wind off the bay. They had been there five minutes or so when a comely woman about Sabina's age stepped up to the rail beside her.

She wore a plaid cape, a white woolen scarf, a small black hat over ash-blond curls; striking white jade pendant earrings complemented the coppery tone of her skin. She leaned forward to scan the crowded wharfside below, caught someone's eye and waved enthusiastically. John had noticed her, too, and was appraising her in typical male fashion. This led Sabina to nudge him sharply with her elbow. He winked at her in return.

The last of the cargo was soon loaded; the deck throbbed with the beat of the engines. Promptly at noon the gangplanks were raised and secured, and several blasts of the ship's horn heralded their imminent departure. When a pilot boat began to ease the *Alameda* away from the wharf, the woman wearing the jade earrings straightened after one last wave and turned so abruptly from the rail that she bumped into Sabina.

"Oh, I'm so sorry," she said.

"Quite all right. No harm done."

"I really should be more careful." Her face was flushed with more than just the cold; the gleam of excitement in her eyes—large brown eyes, the pupils as round as chocolate drops—attested to that. "It's just that I'm happy to be going home."

"You live in Hawaii then?" Sabina asked, smiling.

"In Honolulu, yes. The Waikiki district." Her answering smile was bright and warm. "You're visiting, are you?"

"Yes. My husband and I."

"Have you been to the Islands before?"

"No, we haven't."

"I envy you the pleasure of seeing them for the first time. Well, I must run, my husband will be waiting for me. Oh, I'm Margaret Pritchard, by the way. Mrs. Lyman Pritchard."

"We're Sabina and John Quincannon."

Mrs. Pritchard said "How do you do?" to John, who bowed in return. Then she asked Sabina, "Are you traveling first-class?"

"Yes."

"We are, too. I'm sure we'll see one another again during the voyage. *Aloha* for now." She hurried away.

"Handsome woman," John said.

"And happily married, from the look of her."

He laughed. "I have eyes only for you, my dear."

"And what big eyes they are, my dear."

As cold as it was on deck, Sabina insisted on remaining at the rail until the steamer passed through the Golden Gate. A hot-coffee thaw, then, followed by luncheon in the dining saloon. Afterward John went to one of the smoking rooms to foul the air with the noxious pipe tobacco he favored, and she returned to their cabin. She was unpacking their trunks when he joined her. Whether on purpose or not, he had an uncanny knack for avoiding prosaic chores.

When she finished, he surprised her by suggesting that they share "a relaxing nap"—a none too subtle euphemism, judging by the gleam in his eye.

"Really, John," she said. "In the afternoon?"

"Why not in the afternoon? You yourself declared that this was to be a second honeymoon."

Well . . . why not, indeed?

The bed was quite comfortable, and there was something about the ship's motion and the gentle throb of its engines that made the bon voyage "nap" especially satisfying—a lovely start to their adventure.

Except for the weather, the first two days at sea continued to meet Sabina's expectations. The sky remained overcast with intermittent showers and the wind blew sharp and cold, canceling deck games and outdoor seating, but there were enough indoor diversions to satisfy her, if not John. He spent much of Sunday studying the dossier on Lonesome Jack Vereen and Nevada Ned Nagle and the information on the Honolulu detective, George Fenner, that the Pinkertons had supplied, reading his favorite volumes of poetry by Walt Whitman and Emily Dickinson, and wandering the decks in spite of the inclement weather.

Sabina, who hadn't packed any reading matter of her own, took refuge in the ship's well-stocked library. One book caught her immediate attention—*The Adventures of Sherlock Holmes*. Among the dozen chronicles of the famous British sleuth's exploits was "The Five Orange Pips," which reminded her of the wedding gift she and John had received from Charles Percival Fairchild the Third, the benignly daft scion of a wealthy Chicago family who imagined himself to be Sherlock Holmes.

The gift had been five tiny white-gold nuggets, no doubt meant to represent five orange pips. In the true account those pips had been omens of death; to Charles the Third's upside-down way of thinking, the five gold nuggets were just the opposite, felicitous omens for the success of their marriage. She had been impressed by the offering, but not John. He couldn't abide the man; "an infernal crackbrain" was the mildest of his descriptions. This was because Charles had rather amazingly proven himself to be a detective of considerable skill in his own right, having outmatched John's deductive prowess on the occasion of their first meeting. Sabina, however, had a soft spot for him. He had helped to bring about the resolution of two of their other investigations, including one in which he was framed for the murder of his wealthy cousin; and before leaving San Francisco for parts unknown he had surprised her with a present of the kitten she'd named Eve.

In the package with the five gold nuggets, which had been mailed from Salt Lake City, Charles had included a note stating that he planned to return to San Francisco shortly—a reunion that Sabina had been looking forward to. But six months had passed and Charles had yet to put in an appearance or to initiate contact again. Had something happened to him? She hoped not. Charles had a mercurial temperament and often acted on sudden whims (something she herself had imprudently done not long ago); he might well have postponed his return visit for some incomprehensible reason, still be in Utah or any of countless other places. She would not be surprised if one day a month or a year from now he walked into the offices of Carpenter and Quincannon, Professional Detective Services—preferably when she was there alone. . . .

On Saturday evening she and John dined by themselves, but when they entered the dining saloon on Sunday all the tables were taken. There was seating at two of the four-person tables, one of which was occupied by Margaret Pritchard, the woman they'd encountered on deck before sailing, and a large, distinguished-looking man some ten years her senior. Mrs. Pritchard spied Sabina and smilingly gestured for her and John to join them.

Lyman Pritchard, it developed, was an executive with J. D. Spreckels and Brothers, agents for several Hawaiian sugarcane plantations and a leading exponent of trade between the United States and the Islands. John D. Spreckels was also the founder and owner of the Oceanic Steamship Company, Sabina knew, which likely meant that the Pritchards were traveling gratis or at a much reduced rate. They visited San Francisco annually for a week of business meetings, get-togethers with old friends, and shopping for items unavailable in Honolulu.

John identified himself and Sabina as owners and operators of "a private consulting service," and neatly forestalled questions about just what sort of consultations they engaged in by revealing that they had been married just six months. Margaret said, "Oh, then this trip is a belated honeymoon?," to which Sabina replied more or less truthfully that it was.

The dinner fare proved to be very good—oysters, Dungeness crab, roast lamb, fresh vegetables, a fruit medley that included pineapple and mango—and the Pritchards were convivial companions. Margaret was genuinely and effusively friendly, her chocolate-drop eyes sparkling when she described the picturesque attractions that awaited them on Oahu—Iolani Palace, Diamond Head, the Manoa and Kalihi valleys, the landlocked bay known as Pearl River. Sabina felt an immediate rapport with her. She liked Lyman, too; it was plain from the attention he paid to his wife that he doted on her. John also found them good company. He was quietly charming, a certain indication that he felt socially at ease.

Margaret again wore the white jade earrings, and beamed when Sabina complimented her on them; they had been an anniversary present from her husband, she said, giving his hand an affectionate pat. He smiled at her, and in a habitual gesture akin to John's whisker-fluffing, ran a long forefinger over his ginger-colored mustache—which he'd grown wide and brushy, Sabina guessed, to compensate for the sparseness of his hair. They had been married nine years, having met in San Francisco on one of Lyman's business trips, and had not as yet been blessed with children.

At the end of the meal, as they lingered over coffee, Margaret asked where they would be staying on Oahu. Sabina said, "We don't know for certain. We decided on the voyage on short notice and have no reservations. The Oceanic agent recommended the Hawaii Hotel and said we shouldn't have any difficulty getting accommodations there."

"Oh, my. The Hawaii Hotel is a decent hostelry, but it is located in Honolulu proper and there are quite a few more visitors than usual these days. The city proper isn't the best place to be just now, I'm afraid."

"The Spanish-American war and increased U.S. military presence, for one reason," Lyman said. "Strained relations with Japan, for another. And there have been public protests against the probable annexation by disgruntled natives loyal to Queen Lili'uokalani."

"Does that mean the city is unsafe?" John asked.

"No, not at all. None of the protests have been violent. Tourists have no cause for concern. That is, as long as they avoid Nuuanu Street and Chinatown after nightfall."

John's ears perked up. Nuuanu Street was where the Honolulu detective, George Fenner, hung his hat and shingle. "Chinatown I can understand," he said, "but why the other?"

"Well, you might say that Nuuanu Street is Honolulu's version of the Barbary Coast. Disreputable saloons and other, ah, businesses that cater to sailors and soldiers."

"Where is it located?"

"Near the waterfront, adjacent to Chinatown. Fortunately the Honolulu Police Station is also situated nearby."

Margaret turned the conversational topic back to lodgings. "The city really is crowded these days," she said, "and the number of available hotel rooms is limited. But there are other available accommodations. Many residents rent rooms to visitors for a nominal fee. We do so ourselves on occasion—not a room but a small guesthouse on our property. You would be welcome to stay with us. Wouldn't they, Lyman?"

"I don't see why not."

Sabina said, "It's kind of you to offer, but we wouldn't want to impose."

"It wouldn't be an imposition," Margaret said. "The guesthouse is a separate unit, so you'd have complete privacy. And we're right on the beach at Waikiki."

"How far from Honolulu proper?" John asked. "I have a business matter to attend to in the city."

Neither of the Pritchards asked him the nature of the business matter; they were not ones to pry, fortunately. Margaret said, "It's three miles from our door to the city center. And there is a trolley stop a short distance from our property."

The invitation appealed to Sabina because of the Waikiki location. John seemed less taken with it because of the distance, short though it was, from Honolulu proper. Acceptance or refusal without discussing it privately would be premature.

Margaret, perceptive as well as gracious, sensed this. "You needn't decide now," she said. "We have only just met, after all. We'll become better acquainted, I hope, before we arrive and you can give us your answer then."

Sabina did become better acquainted with the Pritchards over the next two days, but John did not. Beginning early Monday morning a pair of fierce back-to-back storms lashed the *Alameda*, roughening the sea and causing the ship to pitch and roll, now and then to plunge and surge like the bucking of a wild horse. The constant upheaval had no appreciable effect on her; its effect on John, however, was severe—surprisingly so, for he had never complained of motion sickness on any of his many trips on bay and river steamers.

Queasiness kept him confined to their cabin, abed much of the time. Their steward recommended raw ginger root as a remedy for seasickness, but when he brought some from the ship's galley John couldn't abide the taste and refused to swallow it. The continual stomach upset made him short-tempered and grouchy—"Restful ocean voyage? Romantic interludes? Faugh!"—and sent Sabina elsewhere in self-defense.

One place she went was the ladies' lounge, where she and Margaret had arranged to meet daily for afternoon tea. The bond of friendship between them grew stronger at the first of these meetings, when Margaret asked if Sabina considered herself a "New Woman," the term used to describe the modern woman who broke with the traditional role of wife and mother by working outside the home, and Sabina emphatically said she did. Margaret, too, believed in the principle, though her own pursuit of emancipation was limited by Honolulu society. She also heartily approved of Sabina's involvement with the woman suffrage movement, which she, too, supported, and commiserated with her over the fact that the California State Woman Suffrage Convention held in San Francisco in November had failed to produce a voting rights amendment to the state constitution.

Sabina had told her of John's struggles with *mal de mer*. "Is he feeling any better today?" she asked when they met on Tuesday.

"I'm afraid not," Sabina said, and added wryly, "Green is not a becoming color on him."

"Poor soul. I know how he feels—I was a bit green myself on my first crossing. It takes a while for some of us to develop what sailors call sea legs. You're fortunate you were born with them."

"Very fortunate."

"Has he been able to eat anything?"

"Broth and a little milk. Nothing solid."

"His appetite will return once the weather clears. We should have calm seas again soon."

Sabina hoped so. For her sake as well as John's.

Margaret's prediction proved true. On Wednesday morning Sabina awoke to a mostly clear sky and a placid ocean. John's color was much better, his mood likewise when he discovered that the queasiness was gone and he was able to be up and about on steady legs again.

They dressed and went for a stroll on the passenger deck. The Pacific was a deep, sunstruck aquamarine, the air warm, the breeze light and bracing. It was not long before John announced that he was famished. He proceeded to eat a gargantuan breakfast and afterward went to smoke his pipe for the first time in two days.

That night his ardor returned as well. Oh, yes, he was his old self again, definitely none the worse for his mini-ordeal.

The skies remained clear, the ocean as flat and smooth as a pane of colored glass, the days and nights growing progressively warmer as they neared their destination. A posted announcement from the captain stated that the steamer was on schedule to arrive in Honolulu Harbor early Saturday morning.

On Friday evening Sabina and John once again dined with the Pritchards. Margaret regaled them with stories of the Polynesian settling of the Islands, of King Kamehameha and the monarchy, of the coming of the missionaries. She was so well versed on the subject of Hawaiian history, Lyman told them, that she served as a volunteer teacher at a school for the young children of Caucasian residents. This made Sabina like her even more.

She and John had discussed the guesthouse invitation, and toward the end of the meal she gave their decision. He preferred to be in Honolulu proper, but she had pointed out that the shortage of hotel accommodations would make it difficult to find lodgings and likely delay his pursuit of the two swindlers. That, the nominal rental fee, and the consideration of her comfort convinced him. They would be staying at Waikiki with their newfound acquaintances.

4

SABINA

The island of Oahu shimmered in dark green splendor as the *Alameda* neared a point of land Margaret identified as Koko Head, once around which Honolulu would be visible. The shimmer was a thin heat haze. As early as it was, the morning was hot, the air humid and breathlessly still, the sky threaded with milky streaks. John had grumbled about the sticky heat while they were dressing in their lightest attire. Where were the soft blue sky, the balmy trade winds she had touted?

Margaret provided the answer when they joined her and Lyman and several other passengers at the starboard deck rail. "Kona weather," she said.

"It comes two or three times a year when the winds turn westerly."

One of the other passengers, a tubby little man in a white linen suit similar to the one Lyman wore, overheard this and saw fit to add, as if delivering a lecture, "The *kona* winds are actually blown-out typhoons that have come up across the equator. They bring heavy rainstorms and now and then cause volcanic eruptions. The Polynesians believed them to be 'sick winds,' that *kona* weather is 'dying weather.'"

"The Polynesians had many superstitions," Margaret said.

"Yes, and some of them are justified."

John, who was perspiring freely, muttered something unintelligible under his breath. Sabina remained prudently silent.

The steamer rounded Koko Head, slowed as it approached the channel entrance to Honolulu Harbor. Sabina was impressed by her first view of the city. Beyond piers and warehouses lining the waterfront, buildings sprawled in a wealth of tropical vegetation backed by a section of higher ground that Lyman identified as Punchbowl Hill. In the far distance stood a majestic mountain range, Tantalus, whose jagged peaks were like a row of sentinels. The shoreline swept southward in a wide crescent, the extinct volcano known as Diamond Head standing guard at its far end.

They weighed anchor just inside the harbor entrance, near a small island—Quarantine Island, Margaret told them, where ships believed to be carrying contagious passengers were detained and isolated. The reason for the stoppage was a routine quarantine inspection. Shortly a launch arrived from the island with a doctor to perform the examination; it did not take long for him to clear the passengers and allow the ship to proceed.

The *Alameda* took her designated place among a number of other vessels—steamers, three-masted barques, a quartet of gunmetal-gray American naval battleships and troop ships—moored at the long line of piers. Passengers disembarked into a shed where they waited for their baggage. It was stifling hot in the shed; the simple act of drawing breath made perspiration flow from Sabina's pores. The Pritchards, happy to be home, seemed not to mind the heat or the waiting.

The baggage was soon carted in and separated. Lyman assigned their trunks, and hers and John's, to a pair of native porters. Immigration was a mere formality; the Pritchards were well known to the inspector, and when Lyman stated that the Quincannons were to be their guests, they were swiftly passed through.

When they emerged from the shed, they and the other arrivals were greeted by a brass band playing Hawaiian music, by young girls (somewhat scantily clad, though not in grass skirts) who draped fragrant hibiscus-flower *leis* around their necks, and by a handsome, smiling Hawaiian of indeterminate age who proved to be the Pritchards' houseman, Alika. The family equipage, a Studebaker carriage with a calash folding top, drawn by a sturdy sorrel horse, awaited them.

Not a single motorcar was in sight. Sabina asked Lyman if horseless carriages had made their appearance on the island.

"No, not yet," he said, "but they will surely be here by the turn of the century. Some residents feel that the machines will spoil this peaceful paradise of ours."

"Yes," Margaret said, "and we are two of them."

Alika saw to the loading of their trunks into a trailer cart attached to the buggy, and they were soon under way. The drive to the Waikiki district was on a well-graded, packed earth roadway, Kalakaua Avenue, that followed the curve of the shoreline. Sections on both sides of the road had a swampy look relieved somewhat to seaward by groves of coconut palms; inland, beyond a line of trolley tracks, were taro patches and rice fields in which Chinese laborers stood toiling in knee-deep water. The sweltering heat was unrelieved by even a slight breeze; the palm fronds and other vegetation hung limp and lifeless. John appeared to be suffering its effects more than Sabina was—he kept shifting position on the leather seat, wiping his brow, tugging at the collar of his white shirt—but he made no verbal complaints.

The swampland eventually gave way to the residential district of Waikiki. Even though it was three miles from the city proper, it was not at all isolated. In addition to the streetcar tracks paralleling Kalakaua Avenue, here, too, were arc light standards and poles strung with electrical and telephone wires. Clearly this was where a portion of Honolulu's wealthy citizens resided; most of the homes visible here and there were large and set on well-landscaped parcels. The Pritchards' was one of these, a square, two-story waterfront house surrounded by an abundance of tropical flora. Access was along a crushed-shell carriageway that looped across the front of the house, then opened into a parking area at the end of which was a shed-like lean-to and stable.

A young bronze-skinned Hawaiian woman dressed in a bright floral-patterned garment appeared as Alika halted the buggy. When they had all alighted, Margaret embraced the girl, spoke to her briefly in her native tongue, and then performed introductions. She was Kaipo, Alika's wife "and the finest cook on Oahu." The girl smiled shyly and said to Sabina and John, "*E komo mai.* Welcome." After which she hurried off on a path that led into the gardens to their left.

"I asked her to prepare the guesthouse," Margaret said. "Alika will bring your trunks. Meanwhile we'll have something cool to drink on the lanai."

The guesthouse was invisible from this vantage point, its location hidden by the lush vegetation. The plantings on both sides made Sabina catch her breath; it seemed that shades of every vivid color in the spectrum were represented. Their mingled scents were as heady as expensive perfume.

The main house was composed of large, airy rooms comfortably furnished in native *koa* woods, the walls decorated with Island paintings and tapestries. The lanai opened off the living room, separated from it by a bamboo curtain; long and wide, screened on three sides, it extended down a slight slope toward the sweep of beach below. The four of them sat out there on rattan chairs and drank iced fruit punch that Kaipo had prepared.

The drinks and the relative coolness of the enclosed lanai relieved some of Sabina's torpor. John looked less wilted, too, but he was still fidgety and his preoccupied expression told her he was thinking of the two swindlers. He confirmed it when Kaipo entered to inform them that the guesthouse was ready for occupancy.

He was the first to stand, after which he rather rudely consulted his watch and then said to the Pritchards, "My apologies, but as I mentioned on the ship there is a business matter I must see to in the city."

Lyman blinked his surprise. "You mean now? But you've only just arrived. Can't the matter wait until Monday?"

"I would rather attend to it today. If you'd direct me to the nearby trolley stop . . ."

"Alika can drive you into the city."

"The trolley will suit me," John said. His reason for declining the drive offer, Sabina knew, was to keep his destination private. "What is the fare?"

"*Umi keneta* Hawaiian, one dime American. You intend to leave right away?"

"As soon as possible."

Margaret said, "At least come see the guesthouse first. Lyman will show you to the trolley stop. Then you'll be sure to find your way back here when you return."

John agreed to that, after which they all trooped outside with Margaret leading the way.

The guesthouse proved to be a simple thatch-roofed structure with a narrow screened porch facing seaward. Purple and red bougainvillea decorated its walls, and it was shaded by a poinciana tree whose wide, spreading branches and flaming red blossoms put Sabina in mind of a gaily colored parasol. The little structure had been built close to a low fence that separated the Pritchards' property from that of their immediate neighbor. Sabina had a glimpse through shrubbery and across an expanse of lawn of the neighboring house. It was not of Hawaiian design, but surprisingly and rather closely resembled one of the Queen Anne homes prominent in San Francisco.

Two spacious rooms comprised the interior of the guesthouse— sitting room with rattan furniture, bedroom whose two beds were covered by mosquito netting. Like the main house, it had been wired for electricity. A large outdoor rain barrel provided fresh water. Sabina found the accommodation charming and said as much. John made a favorable comment as well, but more out of politeness than with any genuine feeling.

When he and Lyman departed, Margaret asked her if she would like to rest or perhaps go for an ocean dip. Sabina opted for the latter; the prospect of a cooling swim was appealing, the more so when Margaret indicated that that was her intention. She unpacked and donned her bathing costume while her hostess went to change. Margaret's costume, white with an orchid design, was more attractive than Sabina's rather plain one. More revealing, too. Some of the women who frequented the California beaches would probably find it scandalous.

The beach was a short distance down the gradual slope. This section of the garden was dominated by mango trees heavy with fruit, and by one bearing long strands of vivid yellow flowers that Margaret identified as a golden shower tree, one of Hawaii's most common and most attractive.

As they neared a gate that gave access to the beach, Sabina spied a man and a woman beyond a low fence bordering the neighboring property. They stood near a similar gate on that side, facing each other, the man with both hands tightly gripping the woman's arms. He seemed to be in the midst of a heated scolding of his companion. She stood stiffly, her blond head tilted to one side as if she disdained looking at him.

When the man heard Sabina and Margaret approaching, he quickly released his hold, squinted in their direction, then said something to the woman that turned her around and sent her back up the incline without a sideways glance. Sabina had a clear look at her then—young, attractive, Junoesque in stature, dressed in a light-colored blouse and skirt.

The man hesitated, looking after her, then walked over to the fence. He was about sixty, tall and spare, with a long saturnine face and a liver-spotted scalp beneath thinning gray hair. Despite the heat, the beige suit he wore was immaculate.

"Hello, Margaret. So you and Lyman are back." His smile was a mouth-stretch that did not reach his eyes. "How was San Francisco?"

"Cold and wet, I'm afraid."

"Better than this miserable heat and humidity."

"Has the *kona* weather been on us long, Gordon?"

"Three days."

"Oh, drat. I was hoping it was nearing an end."

"We're in for another four or five before the trades begin again." His gaze shifted to Sabina in an appraisal she found too bold for a man twice her age. "Who is this attractive young woman?"

Margaret introduced them. He was Gordon Pettibone, owner of the neighboring property. He allowed as how it was a pleasure to make Sabina's acquaintance, a statement she pretended to share. Her years of detective work had taught her to trust first impressions, and there was something about Mr. Pettibone that left her cold.

Ever polite, Margaret said to him, "We'll be having tea on the lanai at five o'clock with Mrs. Quincannon and her husband. Would you and Philip care to join us?"

"I wouldn't mind," he said, his eyes still on Sabina. "Philip is out somewhere but he'll come if he returns by five."

"Miss Thurmond is welcome, too, if you would like to bring her."

"I think not. She will be busy." He essayed a slight bow, then followed the path the young woman had taken toward the Queen Anne replica.

Sabina said as she and Margaret stepped down onto the white sand beach, "You seemed surprised that Mr. Pettibone accepted your invitation."

Margaret nodded. "He isn't the most social of men. Or very fond of our island, I'm sorry to say."

"Is that why he had his home built to resemble one in San Francisco?"

"It is. He's not a bad neighbor, though he can be standoffish at times. I hope you don't mind that I asked him and his nephew to tea."

"Not at all." Which wasn't exactly the truth.

Mr. Pettibone, Margaret explained then, was the minority owner and head of the Honolulu branch of Great Orient Import-Export, a large firm that dealt in silk, foodstuffs, and other goods from China and the Far East. Philip was Philip Oakes, his nephew and an employee of the firm; the blond woman he'd been scolding was Miss Thurmond, his secretary. Both lived with him. Earlene Thurmond's duties included cataloguing Mr. Pettibone's large collection of books on Chinese history and assisting him on a scholarly tome he was writing on that nation's ancient dynasties. Sabina thought she detected a faint note of disapproval in Margaret's use of the word "duties," as if she suspected the relationship between the two to be more than just employer-employee. The little scene by the gate suggested the same to Sabina.

The white-sand beach was sparsely populated, most of those present children of various ages, and the shade cast by tall palms kept it from being unbearably hot. The cream-tipped rollers were gentle, the water warm and gloriously soft. Sabina's only regret, while she and Margaret bathed, was that John was not here to share her enjoyment. She hoped he had made contact with George Fenner and it proved fruitful, and that he would return before five o'clock. She did not relish the thought of having to socialize with Gordon Pettibone without him.

5

QUINCANNON

The trolley rattled through the swampy lowlands, then ran inland between rows of coconut palms. It stopped often to take on or disgorge passengers of half a dozen or more races, very few of them Caucasian; the slow progress and the oppressive heat inside the car did nothing to improve Quincannon's disposition.

So this was Hawaii, the Crossroads of the Pacific, the place Sabina had quoted Mark Twain as describing in one of his notebooks as "the most magnificent, balmy atmosphere in the world—ought to take dead men out of grave." Smiling native girls in little more than grass skirts and flower *leis*? The only ones he'd seen so far that even came close to fitting that description had been those waiting outside the pier shed; and they, like all the women on this infernal trolley, were well covered. The men were even more stoic, baring their teeth only in panting frowns. One burly fellow, in fact, seemed to study Quincannon's neck as if measuring it for a noose or a knife blade.

Paradise?

Bah!

He focused his thoughts on Lonesome Jack Vereen and Nevada Ned Nagle. He had considered canvassing the hotels for them but discarded the notion. It was not likely the unholy pair would have taken rooms in one, even if the present lack of hotel space in Honolulu permitted it. Their modus operandi was to arrange for private lodging places while working one of their swindles; that was what they had done during the bilking of R. W. Anderson, and they would surely have followed suit here if they were setting up another con. A hotel canvass would be a waste of valuable time, not to mention a daunting task for a stranger in this strange land.

No, his best course of action, like it or not, was to enlist the aid of George Fenner. According to the information supplied by the Pinkertons, Fenner was both an experienced and a competent detective. Until three years ago he had been a member of the Honolulu constabulary, under the authority of the marshal of the kingdom of Hawaii. He had been a security officer in the entourage accompanying Kalakaua, the last king of Hawaii, who had visited San Francisco in 1891 and had eventually died there. When the Sandwich Islands Kingdom breathed its last, two years later, Fenner had supported Marshal Charles B. Wilson in refusing for several hours to turn over the police station to the new provisional government, an act of insubordination that had cost him his job and led him to open his own investigative service.

All of this spoke well of him, but a man's past history could be misleading. This was especially true, in Quincannon's experience, of flycops in general. What was Fenner like today and in person? Would he be willing and able to do Quincannon's bidding at a reasonable price? Yes, and if so how long would it take him to produce results?

The trolley finally turned on King Street and entered the city proper, passing a massive concrete-faced structure set inside a broad square that must be the Royal Palace. Despite the *kona* weather, the cobblestone street was crowded with buggies, men on horseback, pedestrians that included uniformed soldiers and American naval personnel. Quincannon joined the foot traffic at the intersection with Bishop Street. The motorman had told him when he boarded that the quickest route to Nuuanu Street was via Merchant Street, which was one block *mauka*—toward the mountains.

Merchant Street turned out to be a narrow little avenue flanked by heavy, square buildings built of stone that had been brought to the islands in the holds of New England windjammers. (Quincannon knew this from the pamphlet Sabina had inflicted on him before their departure.) The Honolulu Police Station was one of them. A sign identified the imposing structure as such; otherwise he would have passed it by without recognition, for there were no uniformed officers in sight. He continued northward beneath the arcades of countinghouses and the Inter-Island Steamship Company building. Few others were abroad here, the packed-earth street mostly deserted.

Nuuanu Street ran along the head of Merchant Street. It, too, was narrow, flanked on the north side by the shabby buildings and temples of Chinatown. Quincannon turned *mauka* again, the correct direction to Fenner's residence according to the building numbers. There was more activity here, though not nearly as much as there would be at night when sailors off ships in the harbor prowled for liquor, games of chance, and soiled doves. Nuuanu was called Fid Street by the locals (this fact courtesy of the Pinkertons), a reference to the seafarer's term for grog; its reputation among sailors as a "Port of Hell" was evidently justified. Bagnios and gambling halls proliferated in the area, as did saloons bearing such names as Royal Union, Ship and Whale, South Seas Taps. By night they would be lantern-lit and boisterous with music, laughter, bawdy talk; by day they had the same tawdry, semi-deserted appearance as their counterparts in the Barbary Coast.

Quincannon passed them all by. If Vereen and Nagle gravitated here, it would be after dark. And a stranger asking questions about them was sure to be met with silence, hostility, or both.

In the next block, adjacent to a saloon whimsically called the Trader's Rest, he came to a two-story clapboard building that housed a sailors' outfitter downstairs and Fenner's office and living quarters upstairs. He climbed a somewhat rickety outside staircase.

Evidently Fenner did not believe in advertising his profession; there was no shingle at the foot of the staircase or on the door at the upper landing.

Two sets of knuckle raps brought no response. Quincannon tried the door latch, expecting it to be locked, but it wasn't. He opened it, stepped into a deserted office that contained a sluggish ceiling fan, a swarm of flies, a jumble of inexpensive furnishings, and a room at the far end separated by a beaded curtain. He called Fenner's name, received no answer to that, either. The only interior sounds were the dull buzzing drone of the flies.

The room's centerpiece was a rattan desk, atop which sat a two-quart tin bucket and a coconut-shell mug. He stepped over to look into the bucket. One-third filled with beer, not stale but fresh; foam and bubbles appeared when he nudged the bucket. So Fenner had been here recently, and it seemed likely that he would be back, else the door would not have been left unlocked. Gone to answer a beer-induced call of nature, mayhap. There would be no indoor plumbing here.

Quincannon resisted an impulse to prowl the premises, sat instead on a wooden chair. He had been marinating in sweat for three or four minutes when the door opened and a large fat man in a rumpled tropical suit entered. The fat man showed no surprise to find that he had a visitor. His only reaction was to say, "Ah," in a raspy voice.

Quincannon rose to his feet. "George Fenner?"

"None other. And you are?"

"Quincannon, John Quincannon. I hope you don't mind my taking the liberty of coming in to wait."

"Not if you're here on business."

"I am. You were recommended to me by the Pinkerton office in San Francisco." He presented Fenner with Carpenter and Quincannon, Professional Detective Services' business card. "As you see, we are in the same profession."

Raisin-like eyes nestled in fat pouches studied the card, then lifted to take Quincannon's measure. What conclusion Fenner came to, if any, remained hidden. He gestured for Quincannon to be seated again, crossed to the desk with the card held between sausage-size thumb and forefinger. He neither waddled nor moved ponderously, but rather with a kind of fluid ease reminiscent of a jungle cat. The chair behind the desk groaned in protest as he settled into it. He must have weighed close to two hundred and fifty pounds and measured an inch or two over six feet. His shoulders were wide, his ovoid head completely hairless except for a thin brown ruff above disproportionately tiny ears. An imposing specimen, even sitting down.

The presence of the bucket of beer and coconut-shell mug had made Quincannon dubious about Fenner's competency. But the man was not drunk, nor even close to it, and the way he moved and the gleam of intelligence in the dark little eyes indicated the presence of a hard shell beneath the coating of lard, a shrewd brain inside the hairless skull.

At length Fenner said, "Well, then. What can I do for you, Mr. Quincannon?"

"I am on the trail of a slippery pair of confidence men who swindled a client of mine. They arrived here from San Francisco one week ago on the Matson steamer *Roderick Dhu*."

"And you've come all the way to Hawaii in pursuit. Your client must be a wealthy man."

"He is. And I am a tenacious detective."

"The best kind. Only just arrived in Honolulu and in need of help in locating them, is that right?"

"It is."

"You haven't been to the police?"

"No. You can guess why, I'll wager."

"I can. A smart decision in any event. They have their hands full now—the coming annexation, the flood of troops bound for Cuba or remaining to protect Pearl Harbor." Neither of which prospect met with Fenner's approval, judging by the slight lip curl that accompanied the words. "I take it a large amount of money is involved?"

"Not so much cash money," Quincannon said, "as other valuable items that might well be in their possession. I would rather not say what the items are nor how much they're worth."

"Once you locate the men and recover the valuables, if you do, what then?"

"Turn them over to the police, of course." He didn't add that he meant only the two grifters; if he did recover the bonds and stock certificates, he would sequester them until they could be safely returned to R. W. Anderson.

Fenner dipped his chins; that statement did meet with his approval. Once a copper, always a copper, Quincannon thought, not necessarily a bad thing if he was in fact competent.

"Why did they choose to come to Hawaii?" the fat man asked. "A long way to travel to spend ill-gotten loot."

"I suspect it was a new and potentially lucrative swindle that brought them."

"But you have no idea what it might be?"

"Not yet."

"What are their names?"

"I'll tell you that, and provide other pertinent information, if we reach an agreement."

The sluggish fan was doing little to alleviate the stifling heat in the room. Trickles of sweat made the remains of Quincannon's left ear itch. Fenner mopped his red face and glistening dome with a bandanna-size handkerchief, then reached for the beer bucket. His jowls quivered slightly when he peered inside.

"Just enough left for two mugs," he said. "Join me?"

"No, thanks."

The refusal was met with a flicker of relief. Fenner filled the coconut-shell mug, emptied half of it in one long quaff. "Beer is my one weakness," he said. "I'm the saloon next door's best customer.

Three buckets a day in this *kona* weather." He paused and then said, "I can drink four and still retain full control of my faculties."

"I don't doubt it," Quincannon said truthfully.

"Well, then. If the two birds you're after are still in Honolulu, I should be able to find them for you *wikiwiki*. If they've gone to another island, or sailed for the Orient or the South Seas, I can find that out *wikiwiki,* too."

"What does '*wikiwiki*' mean?"

"Speedily. Do they know you've trailed them here?"

"No. They can have no idea of it."

"No more than two days, then, as long as they haven't gone into hiding for some other reason. Longer, in that case. Satisfactory?"

"Yes. And the cost?"

"My fees are reasonable, but I'll need an advance."

"How large an advance?"

"The charge for one day's work. Forty dollars, American."

Reasonable enough, as long as it could be charged to R. W. Anderson for reimbursement. Though if Fenner was more than two days on the job, his fees would make serious inroads in the amount of cash he and Sabina had brought with them.

"Agreed," he said.

"Now I'll have their names."

"Jackson Vereen, known as Lonesome Jack, and E. B. Nagle, known as Nevada Ned. Those are their real names. The aliases they used to buy steamer passage are James A. Varner and Simon Reno. Likely they'll still be using them here."

"Descriptions?"

Quincannon provided them in detail. He emphasized the likelihood that the pair had sought private rather than hotel accommodations, provided the fact that Nagle was a morphine addict who might need to procure more of the drug if the supply he brought with him should run out, and finished by saying, "They may have frequented the local saloons and bagnios since their arrival, but not more than a sampling if they're pursuing a new swindle."

"What type of swindle do they specialize in?"

"Fake stocks when they can find a suitable mark, but they'll work any con that has a substantial payoff. Whatever scheme brought them here has to have that kind of potential."

"So it would seem."

Quincannon said, "You should have enough to go on now, Mr. Fenner. Can you get started right away?"

"As soon as you leave. Where are you staying?"

"In Waikiki, with a couple named Pritchard my wife and I met on the ship. They invited us and she talked me into accepting."

Fenner elevated a thick eyebrow. "You brought your wife along on a hunt for two crooks?"

"She is also my business partner, a former Pinkerton operative and a detective the equal of any man." His tone and narrowed eye challenged Fenner to make an issue of this.

The fat man merely shrugged. "I don't know the Pritchards. Their address?"

Quincannon had gotten it from Lyman and repeated it.

"I'll get a message to you as soon as I have news," Fenner said. "But you'll have to come here to collect it and pay the balance owed in full. Satisfactory?"

"Satisfactory."

Quincannon paid him the forty-dollar retainer in greenbacks. They shook hands—Fenner's was rough-skinned and surprisingly dry—after which Quincannon went to the door. As he let himself out, he saw the fat man rising to his feet. True to his word to immediately commence earning his fee. Either that, or he was on his way to the Trader's Rest to replenish the empty bucket.

6

SABINA

It was just past four o'clock when John returned. He looked as limp, damp, and wilted as his clothing, but he was in better spirits. The meeting with George Fenner, which he related in some detail, had been more encouraging than he'd expected. Still, he was not completely convinced that it would take Fenner no more than two days to learn the whereabouts of Lonesome Jack Vereen and Nevada Ned. "I'll believe it when and if it happens," he said. That was John—skeptical by nature of any investigator other than himself and his partner, particularly one who was unknown to him and whose abilities were as yet unproven.

While he was changing into a fresh suit, Sabina told of her chance meeting with the Pritchards' neighbor, Gordon Pettibone. She made no mention of Mr. Pettibone's rather lecherous appraisal of her in her bathing costume; it would only have aroused John's jealousy and predisposed him to scowl and snap at the man when they met. As it was, he was not keen on having tea with strangers. Or tea at all, for that matter. He considered it unpalatable, had flatly refused to drink the weak tea with milk the steward had brought during his bout with seasickness. The only beverages he cared for were coffee and warm clam juice, the latter a drink *she* found unpalatable.

Gordon Pettibone and his nephew were already present with Margaret and Lyman when Kaipo showed her and John onto the lanai. It did not take long after the introductions for her to decide that Philip Oakes was as unlikable as his uncle. He was a slender, dapper person midway through his thirties, clad in a cream-colored suit with knife-crease trousers and a paisley cravat. He had slicked-down sandy hair, a thin mustache, an air of self-importance, and an annoying habit of repeating every third or fourth sentence as if he suspected his listeners of being hard of hearing. In his youth he probably would have cut a handsome figure, but telltale signs of dissipation suggested a chronic overindulgence in alcohol.

Mr. Pettibone was more sedate in his attitude toward Sabina after meeting John, whose size and demeanor brooked no familiarities with his wife. Philip Oakes, on the other hand, was not as perceptive as his uncle. From the gleam in his shiny blue eyes Sabina could tell that he was one of those lecherous wolves who, upon meeting an attractive woman, immediately imagines her without a stitch of clothes on. He continued to openly ogle her even after being informed that she was a bride of just six months, and seemed either oblivious to or uncaring of John's displeasure. To avoid any unpleasantness she maintained an aloof attitude, speaking to him only when absolutely necessary.

The table around which they sat had been set with a silver tea service, a tray of canapés, and another tray that held a bottle of scotch whiskey and a soda siphon to accommodate Pettibone and Oakes. The latter saw fit to accommodate himself two more times during the ensuing hour, and would have done so a third time if his uncle hadn't stayed his hand with a sharp look and an even sharper "No, Philip." The only indication of the liquor's effects on him was an increased tendency to express and repeat himself at length.

Inevitably he asked after their business interests. John gave him the same answer he had the Pritchards, that they owned a private consulting firm. But that was not enough to satisfy him.

"You and the lovely Mrs. Quincannon both? Really? What sort of consulting do you do?"

"We would rather not discuss the particulars."

"Oh? Very hush-hush, eh? Very hush-hush? It wouldn't involve government work, by any chance?"

"It has in the past, yes, as a matter of fact."

"And occasionally still does," Sabina added.

Evasive answers, but with truthful foundations. Their investigations were indeed private and often hush-hush at the request of their clients. John had served as an operative of the United States Secret Service for a number of years, and just recently, as a favor to his former superior, the head of the Service's San Francisco office, he had been instrumental in breaking up a new and insidious counterfeiting scheme.

Mr. Oakes soon lost interest in them, fortunately, except for an occasional half leer at Sabina. He and his uncle dominated the conversation thereafter, often enough with bits and pieces of information about themselves. Gordon Pettibone had been one of the founders of the Great Orient Import-Export Company in San Francisco in the early eighties and had moved to the Islands after the death of his wife, eight years before. Philip, his late sister's son, had joined him here two years ago after some sort of business failure in Los Angeles. Neither seemed to hold the other in very high regard. Judging from little asides and innuendoes delivered by each, Mr. Oakes considered his uncle a penny-pinching autocrat, while Mr. Pettibone thought his nephew weak-willed and foolish.

When they weren't discussing themselves or each other, they held forth on what was obviously their second favorite conversational topic—the coming U.S. annexation. Gordon Pettibone was all in favor of it; it was bound to increase the Far East trade and the profits therefrom, he said in vociferous tones, and serve to bring in more "good American business interests to help civilize this heathen place." Most of the other American and European residents also supported annexation, Lyman among them, though his position was more moderate; unlike Pettibone, he had not been a staunch supporter of the Reform Party of the Hawaiian Kingdom or a member of the Committee of Safety that had deposed the queen and overthrown the kingdom five years ago.

Philip Oakes, on the other hand, was against the annexation, whether in principle or simply because it nettled his uncle Sabina couldn't tell. He preferred the Islands just the way they were, he said, not overrun with tourists and opportunists who would change both the face and character of them. Margaret agreed with him. So, for that matter, did Sabina, though she kept the opinion to herself. John had nothing to say, either; it was plain to her, if not to any of the others, that he was hardly even listening.

It was a relief when Pettibone and Oakes took their leave—the former after declining Margaret's invitation that they stay for a traditional Hawaiian dinner, the latter after a clumsy attempt to kiss Sabina's hand that she avoided. Once they were gone Lyman said to John, apologetically, "I'm afraid our neighbors can be a bit hard to take at times. I hope you and Sabina weren't too uncomfortable."

"Not at all," he lied.

"I must say I'm relieved they didn't stay to dinner. Margaret, why did you invite them?"

"Well, I was sure Gordon wouldn't accept—he loathes Hawaiian food."

Sabina said, "He doesn't seem to like native Hawaiians very much, either."

"I'm afraid he doesn't, and I can't imagine why—they're wonderful people. His houseman, driver, and groundskeepers are all Chinese. So are all the non-Caucasian employees of his firm."

A racist, Sabina thought, in addition to his other unpleasant character traits. It must be something of a chore for the Pritchards, Margaret especially given her passion for the Islands and their indigenous people, to have men like Pettibone and his nephew residing in such close proximity.

Dinner, prepared by Kaipo and served by Alika on the lanai, was quite to her liking. It consisted of several dishes with exotic names—a noodle soup called *saimin,* chicken with pineapple, shrimp in coconut milk, and *haipu,* a coconut pudding, for dessert. A traditional dish called *poi,* a thick brownish paste made from mashed taro root and eaten by using one's index and middle fingers as a scoop, was her least favorite—an acquired taste that she might but John would never acquire. His horrified expression after one scoop made both Margaret and Lyman laugh.

Coffee and a pipe for John, a cigar for Lyman completed the meal. But they didn't tarry long past sunset. The night had become very humid, very still; even the sea and land birds were quiet. The stillness and a palpable electric current in the dead air presaged a coming *kona* storm. Just how fierce it would be was impossible to predict.

The first thing John said when he and Sabina entered the guesthouse was "It may have been a mistake lodging here."

"Why? Are you concerned about the storm?"

"No, no, that's not the reason."

"What, then? The three-mile trolley ride into the city?"

"Not that, either. The trolley is tolerable."

"So are these accommodations—more than tolerable. And the Pritchards are splendid hosts."

"Yes, but their neighbors leave a great deal to be desired. Especially that crapulous fop Oakes. He kept looking at you the way a fox looks at a sitting hen."

"Really, John. A hen?"

"You know what I mean. As if he'd like nothing better than to eat you."

She laughed. "His first attempted bite would be his last."

"He's a cussed rake. I don't like or trust rakes."

"You were a bit of one yourself, once upon a time," she reminded him.

"Never with another man's wife," he said, scowling. "He had better not make advances to you when I'm not here."

"He won't, he wouldn't dare."

"Don't be too sure."

"But I am sure," Sabina said. "He may be a rake but he's not a nitwit. He knows the Pritchards wouldn't stand for a guest being subjected to that kind of funny business. Neither would his uncle, for that matter. Mr. Pettibone rules him with an iron hand."

"I didn't like Pettibone, either. Blasted self-important windbag."

And a Lothario himself despite his age, Sabina thought, assuming he and the comely Miss Thurmond were in fact cohabiting. Lechery must be an inherited family trait. A good thing John had not been present to witness the way Pettibone looked at her at their first meeting.

"Well, you needn't be concerned about me," she said. "You know perfectly well I can take care of myself in any situation."

He admitted the truth of that.

"Subject closed. Shall we go to bed now? It has been a long day and we both need sleep."

They did not get very much of that needed sleep. The *kona* storm struck in the dead of night, a sudden onslaught of heavy rain and howling wind that immediately woke her. John, too, and he was usually a heavy sleeper. The continual ferocity of the blow kept them awake until it finally began to abate some three hours later. They both slept again then, Sabina fitfully. When she awoke to gray daylight, her nightdress and the bedsheets were sodden with perspiration. The storm had failed to ease the sticky heat; if anything, it had left the air even more sultry—so much so that Sabina felt as though she were trying to breathe under water.

John was still mired in restless slumber. She drew back the mosquito netting, washed from a basin of fresh water, dressed in her thinnest blouse and skirt, and went out onto the screened porch. The sky was the color of dull pewter, though no more rain clouds were visible overhead or on the horizon. Trees and other vegetation glistened wetly in the morning light, still monotonously shedding droplets of rainwater. The path that led to the main house was strewn with leaves, pieces of fruit, a torn-off palm frond. Far out near the reef she glimpsed high, foaming waves. The panorama, so pleasant the day before, was now mildly depressing.

She was sitting lethargically in one of the rattan chairs when their hostess appeared to see how they had fared. Margaret was as smilingly cheerful as ever; Sabina had to make an effort to match her good humor. The storm had not been as powerful as it might have seemed, she reported; the damage it had done to the property was minimal. Her answer, when Sabina asked if there might be other storms before the end of the *kona* cycle, was "It's likely, yes. But perhaps not as severe."

Her suggestion for dealing with the present enervating humidity was to remain quietly inactive. That was what she and Lyman intended to do even though they were acclimated to it. Later, perhaps, they could all go for a swim if the surf gentled enough to permit it.

Kaipo brought breakfast, but Sabina had little appetite and only picked at it. She did read the copy of one of Honolulu's newspapers, The *Pacific Commercial Advertiser,* that Kaipo also brought. There was much in it about the Spanish-American war, though the news from Cuba was several days old and not enlightening; the primary focus, naturally, was on the comings and goings of American warships, the arrival of a garrison of troops at Pearl Harbor and their effect on the local economy.

John, when he finally awakened, was no more interested in food than she and not at all interested in the newspaper. He was in a grumpy mood—the storm, his restless sleep, the sweltering heat, and especially the lack of a message from George Fenner. He knew it was too soon to expect it—it was Sunday, after all—but he was impatient nonetheless. He was not good at waiting at the best of times, and dependence on someone he barely knew for vital information made him even more anxious.

The morning crawled away. She and John seldom lacked the ability to communicate, but they had little enough to say to each other today. The *kona* weather seemed to have temporarily robbed them of even mundane conversational topics. After a time the torpor Sabina felt gave way to drowsiness; she went into the bedroom, lay down on the now-dry sheet in her bed, and was soon asleep. At some point John had come in, too; he was snoring gently in the other bed when she awoke.

It was midafternoon then, the air a trifle more breathable. She went to look outside. The pale orb of the sun appeared, disappeared, reappeared among shifting cloud formations driven by high-altitude winds. From what she could see of the ocean, the incoming surf was no longer unsettled and should be calm enough for bathing.

John roused as she was putting on her costume. Normally he avoided athletic pursuits such as swimming, but like her he was moist and prickly-skinned after his nap, and the prospect of a cooling dip appealed to him, too. He thought he looked foolish in his blue pin-striped costume—"a half-naked hairy ape" was how he described himself—but Sabina's opinion was that he cut a rather dashing figure.

There were a few people on the beach, mostly sun-browned native children playing in the sand and a few adults prowling among the piles of driftwood and other detritus that had been cast up by the storm. The ocean, which she and John quickly entered, was a welcome respite from the heat despite its bathwater temperature. Actual swimming required too much effort; mostly they just splashed about, letting the rollers wash over them.

After a time, refreshed, she went to dry off in the shade of a coconut palm while John continued to bathe. She noticed then that a fully dressed Caucasian woman had joined the natives on the beach, and despite the wide floppy straw hat the woman wore Sabina recognized her as Gordon Pettibone's secretary. Miss Thurmond wandered among the piles of flotsam and jetsam, apparently not in search of shells, for she picked none up. Nor anything else until something caught her eye and she pounced on it like a cat pouncing on a mouse.

The woman was too far away for Sabina to tell what the object was, only that it was small and dark-colored. Miss Thurmond examined it briefly, then put it into a pocket of her beige dress and hurriedly left the beach. Sabina's impression was that Miss Thurmond had not been randomly beachcombing, that she had been searching for whatever it was that she'd finally found.

The message from George Fenner arrived shortly past nine on Monday morning. She and John were just finishing breakfast when Alika brought the sealed envelope. It was slightly less steamy hot today, a light ocean breeze having begun to intermittently rattle tree branches and palm fronds, and they had both recovered some if not all of their appetites.

John's entire demeanor changed when he tore open the envelope and read what was written on the sheet of paper inside. Whereas he had been half fidgety, half listless before, now he was animated again. His voice resonated with controlled enmity when he said, "Fenner located Vereen and Nagle. True to his word, by Godfrey!"

"Where are they?"

"The note doesn't say. He'll tell me in person."

He showed her the paper. Back-slanted printed words read succinctly: *Have requested information. Office open until 1 p.m.* Then he folded it, tucked it into a trouser pocket, and went inside.

Sabina followed him into the bedroom, watched as he unpacked and loaded his Navy Colt. "I hope you don't have to use that," she said.

"So do I."

"It could mean serious trouble if you do. We have no legal jurisdiction here."

"No, but a citizen's arrest is legal anywhere with just cause. So is self-defense."

He put the pistol into a belt holster, strapped it on, donned a jacket to cover it, kissed her briefly, and went off to put what she fervently hoped would be a swift, safe end to his quest.

7

QUINCANNON

Lonesome Jack Vereen and Nevada Ned Nagle, who were still using the aliases James Varner and Simon Reno under which they'd sailed, had procured a small bungalow on the lower slope of Punchbowl Hill, not much more than a mile from Nuuanu Street.

According to Fenner's investigation, the pair had not indulged their vices by frequenting the Fid Street saloons or the Chinatown brothels during the past week. But they had spent one evening shortly after their arrival in one of Honolulu's better resorts, in the company of a Big Island (the local name for the island of Hawaii) ranch owner named Stanton Millay, the three of them ruining their gizzards with large quantities of a potent Hawaiian liquor called *okolehao*.

The fact that the two thieves had mostly chosen a sub-rosa lifestyle was a sure sign that they were involved in another large-scale swindle. Millay might be their new mark, but if so, the game must be something other than one of their favorite stock grifts; the rancher, according to Fenner, was not the sort to have anything to do with the stock market. Well, the nature of the flimflam, whatever it was, would be revealed soon enough.

Quincannon rented a roan saddle horse at the same livery that had supplied Vereen and Nagle with a horse and buggy, and rode to Punchbowl Hill following the directions Fenner had given him. The fat man had offered to accompany him, but Quincannon neither wanted nor needed assistance in putting the arm on his quarries. Besides, he was loath to pay Fenner another forty-dollar day wage.

It took him nearly an hour to find Hoapili Street and the right bungalow, for the streets in the area had been laid out in a confusing hodgepodge and not all the dwellings bore clearly numbered addresses. Once he was certain he had the right address, he rode slowly past with the brim of his hat pulled down low to shield his face.

The bungalow was half hidden behind tall hibiscus shrubs and a cluster of stubby palms. There was no sign of the rented horse and buggy. One of the grifters might still be here, however, the other off on some sort of errand; it would make his task easier if so. If both were absent, he would wait for their return no matter how long it took.

He picketed the horse behind the concealing branches of a thorn-laden tree, wiped his dripping face with an already damp handkerchief. The heat was intense again today, the sticky air dead still, the sky once more coated with a milky, shimmering radiance that burned the eye. Riding in the open squeezed out a constant trickle of sweat that itched his beard, plastered his shirt to his skin. Even the grip of the Navy Colt felt moist when he touched it.

He paused beside the tree to once again examine the area. Two other bungalows were within sight, these also roofed with palm-leaf thatch and hemmed in by jungly vegetation. The only sign of life anywhere was a scruffy mongrel dog panting in a patch of shade across the roadway. Vereen and Nagle were both night creatures by nature and preference, not unlike the vampires of legend; if one of them were to be in residence at this hour of morning, likely he would be asleep or half comatose with drink or drug.

Quincannon adjusted the Navy's holster until it rode more comfortably on his hip. Then he set off down the road, keeping to pockets of shade wherever possible. The line of hibiscus along the rear side of the bungalow afforded enough cover that he was able to approach it on a more or less straight trajectory. When he reached the shrubs he moved along parallel to them, through tall grass, until he came to a point where the flowered tangle grew thinly enough for him to see through.

Unrolled bamboo blinds covered a single window in the side wall. Along the front, part of an overgrown lanai was visible. He stood listening. The stillness remained unbroken.

He made his cautious way around to the rear, past the bushes to where a privy leaned and a grouping of mango trees overpowered the hibiscus with the odor of overripe fruit. The back entrance had two doors, the outer one screened and the inner one open for ventilation. He allowed a brief, feral grin to split his whiskers, then drew the Navy and waded quietly through a patch of high grass to the screen door.

It was not latched. He eased it open an inch or two; the hinges made no sound. He widened the gap just enough to edge his body through, let the door whisper shut again behind him.

He was in a small kitchen all but filled by a table and chairs and a primitive cast-iron stove. The table and the stovetop were littered with unwashed dishes and remnants of food a-crawl with insects; the two thieves were of the type who maintained personal tidiness while permitting their surroundings to descend into chaos.

Trapped heat made the place a sweatbox; Quincannon's face and body were dripping again as he entered the empty and equally disarrayed room beyond—a small sitting room that opened into a screened side porch. The stale air in there reeked of a combination of cheap tobacco—Vereen was fond of long-nine cigars—spicy food, a sweetish flower essence, and unwashed bodies. Among the clutter he spied the wilted remnants of a flower *lei*, and on the arm of a rattan chair, a length of brightly colored tapa cloth such as he'd noticed native women used to bind their breasts. The cloth was the source of the flower essence. Vereen and Nagle might not have sampled the fare in the Fid Street brothels, he thought sardonically, but arrangements had evidently been made for them to be serviced here.

Opposite the porch entrance was a bead-curtained doorway. Quincannon parted the beads, being careful to keep them from rattling as he stepped through into the short hallway beyond. A pair of bedrooms opened off it, their entrances also curtained. He eased his head through the beads on the left. That room was empty, neither clothing nor luggage in evidence. He crossed to the other bedroom.

The smell that assailed him when he neared the curtain there was far more unpleasant than those elsewhere in the bungalow—one from past experience he knew all too well.

He said aloud, explosively, "Damnation!"

There was no longer any need for stealth; he shouldered through the curtain, causing the beads to click violently. The source of the smell lay atop a bamboo-framed daybed—Nevada Ned Nagle, eyes like blue-glass prisms staring sightlessly at the ceiling.

Holstering the Navy Colt, Quincannon covered his nose and mouth with his handkerchief as he approached the bed. Nagle's plump, fully clothed body had a bloated look, the slack lips and spiky imperial a nest of feeding insects. Dead at least a day. The corpse bore no marks of violence. A fatal coronary? Possibly, but the faint bluish tint to the facial skin was indicative of a morphine overdose.

Nagle had fed his addiction by injections of morphine sulfate; one ampoule lay on the bed next to him, a syringe and two ampoules on the bedside table. Accidental overdose, if that was the cause? Or had Vereen done away with him? The two had been partners for some time, but for men like them there was no such thing as loyalty or lasting friendship. The spoils from the Anderson swindle had not been enough to trigger mayhem in California, but if the potential profit in the new swindle was great enough, Lonesome Jack was not above a lethal double cross in order to claim all the spoils for himself.

Searching the remains was a disagreeable but necessary task.

Nagle's trouser pockets contained a filigreed gold pocket watch with a heavy gold chain and elk's-tooth fob, the watch's inside lid bearing an inscription that read TO HAROLD FROM HIS LOVING WIFE (Nagle's given name was Edwin and he had never been married); a leather case in which was another vial of morphine ampoules; and a purse with a few small coins but no specie or greenbacks. The shirt pocket was empty. A frock coat, much too heavy for this tropical climate, was draped over a chair at the foot of the bed. Its pockets yielded nothing of interest.

As Quincannon was about to re-drape the coat, his fingers encountered something that crinkled in the lining of one of the tails. An examination of the lining revealed a hidden pocket into which a folded piece of paper had been sewn a map, crudely hand-drawn in india ink.

The map depicted the outline of an island with an irregular coastline. One of the Hawaiian islands, evidently. It was not named, but printed in a crabbed hand along the left-hand edge were several labeled X's: Kawaihae, Puako, Auohe, Waimae Pt., Kailua. The X that bore the name Auohe was heavily inked and circled.

Quincannon pocketed the map. The odor of decay was having a nauseous effect on his stomach. Quickly he looked through the two carpetbags in the room, both of which belonged to Nevada Ned. Neither contained anything of importance.

He went across to the other bedroom. Nothing belonging to Vereen remained there. A quick search, then, of the bungalow's other two rooms. Nothing. The stock certificates and bearer bonds belonging to R. W. Anderson, and however much stolen cash was left . . . gone.

One thing was certain: whether or not Lonesome Jack was responsible for his partner's demise, he would not be returning here— not even to dispose of the corpse, were he so inclined, because of the risk involved. Wherever he'd gone, he was sure to be in a hellacious hurry to complete the swindle that had brought them to Honolulu and make his escape.

Glowering, Quincannon left the bungalow as he'd entered it and made his way along deserted Hoapili Street to where he'd left the horse. The glower held fast during the ride back to the city center. An affront, that was what this investigation had become—a continual, galling, personal affront. Vereen must not get away from him again!

8

QUINCANNON

George Fenner's Fid Street office was closed. And his return was not imminent, else the door would have been left unlocked. Gone off on business? Or to slake his beer thirst or to fill his gullet with food? In no frame of mind to wait passively, Quincannon went in search of him.

The fat detective was not in the Trader's Rest saloon next door, nor had he been there this morning. The bartender allowed as how he might be found at this hour in his favorite Chinatown feeding place and provided directions. The dimly lit restaurant, in a narrow alley not far from Nuuanu Street, was where Fenner was, right enough, seated in a private alcove behind a flagon of beer, a mound of fried rice, and a dish of something that looked suspiciously like the cut-up tentacle of an octopus swimming in its own ink.

He didn't ask how Quincannon had located him. Professional courtesy, perhaps. His greeting, spoken through a mouthful of rice: "Back so soon? The two *kukas* must not have been at the bungalow."

Quincannon sat in a spindly chair across from him. "One of them was," he said in a lowered voice. "Nevada Ned Nagle."

"And you didn't put him under citizen's arrest?"

"Not much point in arresting a dead man."

"Dead?" Fenner paused in the act of spearing a chunk of tentacle. "By your hand?"

"No. Either by his own, unintentionally, or his partner's. An overdose of morphine."

"How long ago?"

"Sometime yesterday and so ripening in the heat."

"No sign of the other one?"

"Not a trace. No luggage, nothing left behind but Nagle's corpse." The fat man set his chopsticks down, dabbed at his lips with his bandanna-size handkerchief, then quaffed deeply from the flagon. Quincannon's mouth and throat were parched from the morning's efforts; he watched Fenner have at his suds with one of the few twinges of envy he'd felt since taking the pledge nearly a decade ago. Also on the table was a glass of water; he picked it up and drained it without asking permission.

Fenner didn't seem to mind. He said, "Nagle's death should be reported to the police."

"Not by me. I can't afford to be held up by official red tape with Vereen still on the loose."

"You think he murdered his partner?"

"Conceivably," Quincannon said. "If he did, it was because the new swindle's cush is much greater than they were used to playing for."

"And you believe it is."

"I do. Whether he succeeds in putting it over or not, I damned well intend to find him before he departs for San Francisco or the Orient."

"You're a hard man when the situation warrants, eh, Quincannon?"

"Not unlike you, I'll warrant."

Fenner's mouth curved slightly, the closest to a smile his poker face would allow.

Quincannon said, "The rancher, Millay, that Vereen was seen drinking with. Is he wealthy enough to be Vereen's mark?"

"Yes. Stanton Millay and his sister Grace own a large ranch on the Big Island. She runs it. He spends much of the profits, and is none too careful how."

"But not in the stock market."

"No. I don't know him personally, but his primary vices are reputed to be women, *okolehao,* and poker."

A poker grift was not in Vereen and Nagle's repertoire. If Millay was their mark, the game had to be something that did not involve gambling. "Do you know if Millay is still in Honolulu?"

Fenner shook his head. "Chances are he's gone back to the Big Island by now. He seldom stays in Honolulu more than a few days."

"Where does he usually lodge here?"

"The Hotel Honolulu. The bar there was where he was drinking with Vereen and Nagle."

"How did you find that out, if you don't mind my asking?"

"The barman is an acquaintance of mine."

"Acquaintance" being a polite term for "informer and information seller"; Fenner must have his share of them here, just as Quincannon did in San Francisco. "Did he happen to overhear any of what the three of them discussed?"

"He didn't tell me if he did."

"Would he talk to me? With your sanction, that is."

"Yes, but not for free. You'll have to pay him."

"I expected as much. His name?"

"Winchell. Oliver Winchell. You won't have any trouble finding him—he's working the day shift this week." Fenner took a business card from his pocket, wrote something on it with the stub of a pencil. "Give him this by way of introduction."

Quincannon pocketed the card without looking at it. "And where is the Hotel Honolulu?"

"On Beretania, off Punchbowl Street."

"If Millay has gone back to the Big Island, by what means? Inter-island steamer, his own boat?"

"Inter-island steamer, as far as I know."

Quincannon did not have to ask where such passage was arranged. He remembered having passed the Merchant Street offices of the Inter-Island Steamship Company on Saturday.

He asked, "What kind of ranch do the Millays have?"

"Cattle. Prime beef."

"A cattle ranch? In Hawaii?"

"There are several large ranches on the Big Island. The Parker ranch is the largest by far—they run more than fifty thousand head. The Millays' ranks fourth or fifth."

"Fifty thousand head?" Quincannon was astonished.

"Thriving cattle business in the islands. Has been for nearly a hundred years."

The fat man picked up his chopsticks, helped himself to the last large chunk of eight-legged sea creature. From the way he chewed it, it must have had the consistency of rubber. Quincannon's stomach muscles twitched. Why subject your innards to something as unappetizing as octopus-in-ink when prime Hawaiian beefsteak was available?

He fished out the crude map he'd found hidden in Nevada Ned's coat. Laid it on the table next to Fenner's plate, and explained where he'd found it. "Would this be a drawing of the Big Island?"

Fenner gave it a quick study, quaffing beer again as he did so. "It would," he said. "Kailua is the largest town on the Kona Coast. Kawaihae and Puako . . . little fishing villages, as I recall. Years since my last visit to that part of the Big Island."

"Is the Millay ranch located there?"

"Inland between Puako and Waimae Point, I think. On the lower slopes of Mauna Kea."

"And *Auohe*?"

"A Hawaiian word that means 'hidden place,'" Fenner said. "As far as I know, there's no village or anything else along that stretch of coast that carries the name."

"You've no idea what it might refer to on this map?"

"None. Unless it marks the location of the ranch road, but I don't see how that would translate to '*auohe*.'"

Quincannon said, "You told me earlier that the owner of the Hoapili Street bungalow is a man named . . . Gomez, was it? Maybe he has the answer."

"Justo Gomez. Half-caste Portuguese-Hawaiian. A *kuka* mixed up in a number of shady enterprises—gambling, prostitution. How Vereen and Nagle made contact with him I don't know."

"Where can I find him?"

"Justo's Bait and Tackle Shop, on the waterfront near River Street."

Quincannon stood up. Fenner said, "One thing to be settled before you leave."

"Yes?"

"Nagle's death has to be reported to the authorities. Matter of public safety. But there are ways for it to be done anonymously and without repercussions."

"By you?"

"For a small additional charge."

Quincannon paid the charge without argument. The outlay of money was not an issue at this point. And he had to admit that if their positions had been reversed, he himself would have expected to be paid for making such arrangements.

9

QUINCANNON

The Hotel Honolulu was not a luxurious hostelry by anyone's definition, though neither was it a low-class establishment. A plain two-story structure, attractive enough without being distinguished, its walls and double-decked balconies painted white and draped with flowering vines. The primary appeal for a wealthy rancher like Stanton Millay must be either a preference for modest accommodations or a fondness for the bar where he had been drinking with Vereen and Nagle.

Stanton Millay had lodged there most of the previous week, a Chinese desk clerk informed Quincannon, but had checked out early Sunday morning. Apparently he had returned home to the Big Island. The question was whether he had gone alone or in the company of Lonesome Jack.

Entrance to the bar lounge was through a beaded archway at one end of the lobby. A wall placard there advertised a nightly show of native Hawaiian dances, featuring one called "the *hula kahiko*." The interior of the resort was a small, dark, stuffy space that opened onto a broad lanai lined with torches. The lanai was where the dances were held, evidently; tables surrounded a central fire pit on three sides, and there was a sandy area decorated with potted palms on the fourth. At this hour there were few customers, almost all of those present seated at the outdoor tables; the only ones at the bar that extended along one wall were a pair of middle-aged men in business suits. The single barkeep moved in indolent shuffles behind the polished plank.

Quincannon stepped to the bar at a point farthest from where the two men had their noses in schooners of beer. The barman approached him with a professional smile of welcome lighting his ruddy cheeks. He was a broad-chested gent, bald except for a tonsure of curly brown hair above a pair of jug-handle ears. The Hawaiian shirt he wore, white with an array of bright orange-colored flowers, reminded Quincannon of one of his own favorite vests—a natty silk number festooned with orange nasturtiums that he seldom wore anymore in deference to Sabina, who considered it gaudy. Not here by comparison, it wouldn't be. But then if he'd worn it in this climate, he would be roasting more swiftly than he already was.

"Yes, sir? Something cool and refreshing, p'raps?"

"Water," Quincannon said.

"Plain water?"

"In a large glass. With ice."

He drained the glass in two swallows and called for a refill, which lasted three swallows. The cold water was much more soothing to his parched throat than the tepid glassful he'd drunk in the Chinese restaurant.

"Hot day, isn't she," the barman said in a marked Australian accent. "*Kona* weather, y'know."

"All too well. You're Oliver Winchell?"

"That I am. And how would you be knowing my name?"

Quincannon laid the business card Fenner had given him on the bar top. He'd looked at what was penciled on the back of it after leaving the restaurant. Just the numeral 6 followed by a star symbol, and below that the initials G.F. A code of some sort that induced an immediate change in the Australian when he saw it. His blandly bored gaze turned shrewd, eager; his shoulders twitched as if shrugging off his barman's persona. He leaned forward, and when he spoke his voice had lowered two octaves and taken on a confidential note.

"What can I do for you, mate?" he said. "Mate" now, not "sir"; the card, in his eyes, had put them on more or less equal footing, as with a couple of soon-to-be conspirators. Quincannon saw no profit in disabusing him of the notion.

"Tell me about Stanton Millay."

"Mr. Millay? A fair dinkum gent. Lodges in our house reg'lar when he's in from the Big Island." Winchell's voice dropped another octave. "Got an eye for a pretty face, he has. Fancies one of the girls wot dances the *hula kahiko*."

That explained the rancher's preference for the Hotel Honolulu. "My interest is in the night a week ago when he was here drinking in the company of two Americans."

"The American gents, eh? Mr. Fenner was by askin' about them just yesterday."

"On my behalf."

"Ah," Winchell said. Then, craftily, "P'raps he told you about the arrangement him and me has. . . ."

Quincannon fished out a silver dollar and put it down on the bar, closer to himself than to the Australian. Winchell eyed it covetously, and in a way that suggested he was thinking of asking for a twin. He would not have gotten it if he had.

"Tell me about that night, Oliver."

"I remember it well. Saturday night, it was, the same day Mr. Millay came back from San Francisco."

". . . He was away in San Francisco?" Winchell must not have told this to Fenner, else the detective would have mentioned it.

"That he was. He travels there sometimes."

"For what reason?"

"Buys cattle, sells cattle, likely—part of his business." Winchell essayed a sly little wink. "Raises a bit of hell there, too, I'll wager. He likes a good time, Mr. Millay does."

"Do you know where he met the two with him?"

"On the ship coming across, eh?"

No, Quincannon thought, it was much more likely that Vereen and Nagle had made Millay's acquaintance in a Barbary Coast saloon or one of the three Uptown Tenderloin fleshpots. That cleared up one point, if so.

"Were you in a position to hear some of their conversation?" he asked.

"Snatches of it here and there when I served 'em, only that. We're always busy here of a Saturday night."

"What were the snatches about?"

"Sheilas, mostly."

"Sheilas?"

"Women." The sly wink again. "Eager to sample the local wares, the two Americans were. Mr. Millay was talkin' up a bawdy house he knows in Chinatown. I don't recall as I heard him say which one—"

"Not important," Quincannon said. "What else did they talk about?"

"Well, I think they might've had a deal on."

"What kind of deal?"

"Sorry, mate, I can't tell you because I didn't hear 'em say what it was. Kept their voices down the one time I come in earshot while they were on about it. Something to do with the cattle business, I reckon."

"Did Millay call either of the Americans by name?"

Winchell started to answer, but one of the men at the other end of the bar interrupted him with a call for another schooner of beer. He said, "Half a mo," and hurried off to comply.

Quincannon waited, drumming fingers on the bar top. A swindle involving the cattle industry? It was possible, he supposed, but it struck him as improbable. Vereen and Nagle would know as little about the cattle business as he did, surely not enough to orchestrate a related con game that would fool a seasoned rancher.

Winchell came back and resumed his confidential pose. "Now what was it you was asking again?"

"If Millay called either of the Americans by name."

"By name. Well . . ."

"Jack or James? Ned? Simon?"

"None of those is familiar. No, I don't recall that any names was used whilst I was near."

"All right. Did Millay bring them back again after that night?"

"No. I never set eyes on 'em a second time. Mr. Millay, he was in most nights last week to see Leilani, the hula dancer." Wink. "He's got good taste in sheilas, he has. Leilani is a sweet little piece."

"Did he have anything to say about the Americans?"

"Only once," Winchell said, "and not much then. Funny, though. I asked him how his American friends were and he said, 'Friends. A poor damn joke that is.' Turnabout from that first night when they was cobbers, eh?"

"Is that all he said about them?"

"That's all. He seemed some devo—upset, like—to have 'em called to mind. Maybe the deal they had on fell through."

Maybe so. But if Millay had seen through the swindle and ditched the pair, why had they stayed on in the Hoapili Street bungalow instead of returning to San Francisco? And why would Nagle keep the crude map sewn into his jacket lining? And where was Vereen now, if not gone to the Big Island with Millay or on his own?

There was no more useful information to be gleaned from Oliver Winchell. Quincannon slid the silver dollar across the bar and the Australian made it disappear with the alacrity of a stage magician performing a conjuring trick. Now you see it, now you don't.

The question of whether Stanton Millay had returned to the Big Island alone or in the company of Lonesome Jack Vereen was largely if not fully answered by a clerk in the office of the Inter-Island

Steamship Company. By claiming that Millay and the pseudony-
mous James A. Varner were business acquaintances, Quincannon
learned that both men had purchased tickets for Kailua on the Kona
Coast on Sunday morning.

The tickets had been purchased separately, however, at different times. Did that mean Millay and Vereen had not been traveling together, or simply that they had arranged to meet on the ship?
And where were they bound once they arrived—the cattle ranch, the
mysterious *auohe*?

Passenger transport to the Big Island was limited to one sailing per day, and this day's ship had already departed. Quincannon
booked cabin passage for himself to Kailua on tomorrow morning's
steamer. The delay chafed at him, but he supposed it was just as well
he was unable to leave immediately. Sabina would be furious if he
were to disappear for an indefinite period with no more explanation
than a brief message. And he would need fresh clothing, his toilet
kit, and extra ammunition for his pistol.

10

The broad sweep of Honolulu Harbor resembled that of San Francisco Bay in the number of vessels anchored offshore and at the long piers. The main difference was the warships here—gunboats and battle cruisers that were part of Admiral Dewey's Asiatic Squadron, refueling and taking on supplies for their passage to Cuban waters. Quincannon had little tolerance for war, and the present one was particularly unpalatable—a tempest in a teapot brewed by Washington bureaucrats and whipped to a frenzy by William Randolph Hearst and Joseph Pulitzer and their rallying cry of "Remember the *Maine*! To Hell with Spain!" as a means of selling their New York newspapers. Warmongering politicians, muckraking journalists . . . a pox on the lot of them.

The naval ships, sailing barques, and other craft all sat motionless on the gunmetal-gray water like toys fashioned from gigantic blocks of wood and metal. A forest of masts pierced a sky that seemed to have been flattened down over the sea beyond the channel entrance. Kanaka stevedores moved sluggishly on the docks, loading and unloading cargo at a retarded pace that would have cost them their pay on San Francisco's Embarcadero. Even the dray horses stood or plodded limply in the sodden heat.

Quincannon again felt as if he were melting by the time he located Justo Gomez's place of business. The torrid weather had dulled his sense of urgency, but his temper was still crimped and primed. Any sort of provocation was liable to set it off.

Justo's Bait and Tackle Shop was a small building on the waterfront, weather-beaten and in ramshackle condition. The heat-thick smells of brine and fish flared his nostrils when he entered. Nets hung dustily from two bare walls. Behind a plank laid across a pair of sawhorses, a man clad in dungarees and a sleeveless shirt sat slouched in a rattan chair with his feet up on the plank. He was short and wiry, dark-skinned, with black hair and black eyes and swarthy features that proclaimed his Portuguese/Hawaiian ancestry. Sweat glistened on his bare shoulders and arms like oil on burnished wood.

Only the black eyes moved as Quincannon approached him. They were shrewd, calculating. After a few seconds of scrutiny, his thin lips parted over as many gold teeth as white in a wily grin.

"*Aloha,*" he said.

"Justo Gomez?"

"Sure, that's me." The grin widened. "Man, you look like you just off some old pirate ship. All that brush you got on your face, somebody ever call you Blackbeard?"

Gomez, it seemed, compensated for his small stature with an aggressive, bullying manner. The snotty rudeness was a splinter-like goad on Quincannon's temper. He was proud of his whiskers; an insult to his facial hair was an assault on his self-esteem.

He said sharply, "No one that ever lived to draw another breath."

The little man lost his grin. He swung his feet off the plank, stood up slowly. "What you want, *haole*? Some kine fella looks like you, dressed like you, ain't interested in fishing."

"Information."

"You come to the wrong place," Gomez said. "Justo sells bait, nets to catch fish. He doan sell information."

A single silver dollar would not have been enough to prime this one's pump, and even if it had been, Quincannon was not inclined to part with any more bribe money. "I'm not buying," he said.

"You want it free? Hah. Justo doan give nothing away free."

"Tell me about Lonesome Jack Vereen."

Gomez's only reaction to the name was a squint of one eye. "Who?"

"Lonesome. Jack. Vereen."

"Never heard of nobody with that name."

"How about James A. Varner?"

"Not him, neither."

"Don't try my patience, Gomez," Quincannon snapped. "You supplied him and his partner with a bungalow on Hoapili Street last week."

". . . Who tole you that?"

"Never mind who told me."

"Who are you, man? Some kine policeman?"

"Close enough. A friend of George Fenner."

"That *hewa*." Gomez shaped a spitting mouth to go with the epithet. "What you want from me, hey?"

"I told you, information."

"Justo got nothing to tell you."

"I think you do."

"You crazy in the head. You want to know about those other two *haoles,* go talk to them."

"Vereen isn't in Honolulu anymore. He went to the Big Island. I want to know why."

"How I gonna know why? Go away, *haole*. Justo doan want you in his shop."

Quincannon had reached the limit of his patience. He had dealt with swaggering crooks like Gomez before, and the only sure way to handle them was with a show of greater aggression. He fixed the half-caste with the basilisk glare that had been the bane of many a lawbreaker, swept the tail of his jacket aside so that his holstered Navy was visible, and stepped up close to the little man. Sight of the weapon widened the black eyes, caused them to wiggle in their sockets.

"Hey," he said, "what kine big gun you got there?"

"You want me to show you, up close?"

"No. No."

"Then answer my questions." Quincannon tapped the Navy's handle with his fingertips. "Tell me about Vereen."

Gomez seemed to be making an effort to swallow his Adam's apple. "I doan know that name, only Varner."

"How do you know him?"

"Him and the fat *haole* come in seven, eight days ago, looking for place to stay. Big *kanaka waiwai,* he send them."

"What does '*kanaka waiwai*' mean?"

"Rich fella. Friend of Justo's."

"Stanton Millay."

"Sure. You know him, what you come to me for?"

"I don't know him, but I will before long," Quincannon said. "Friend of yours, is he? What do you do to curry his favor, supply him with women?"

"Hey, what you think Justo is?"

"I know what Justo is. You supplied Vereen and his partner with women, too, didn't you?"

"I doan know what you talking about."

"The devil you don't. Where and how did those two get together with Millay?"

"I doan know."

The repetition of Gomez's favorite phrase led Quincannon to lift the Navy partway out of its holster. He held it there meaningfully, then let it slide back down, but he kept his hand on the handle. And added a little more candlepower to the fierceness of his glare.

Gomez's eyes wiggled again and he said quickly, "Some kine place in San Francisco, that's where they meet."

"What kind of business deal have they got cooking with Millay?"

"I doan know. They doan tell Justo nothing."

"But you know there is a deal," Quincannon prodded, "I can see it in your face. How do you know?"

"Something I hear the fat *haole* say to the other one. That clock gonna make us rich, he say."

"Clock? What kind of clock?"

"Maybe not clock, maybe cloak. Justo ain't sure."

"Does either mean anything to you?"

Gomez wagged his head.

"Is that all you overheard?"

"That's all. Other one shut him up quick, you bet."

Clock or cloak . . . neither seemed to fit the established pattern of a Vereen and Nagle swindle, though with those two anything was possible if there was enough profit to be had. Gomez's eyes said he wasn't lying, but he might have misheard.

Quincannon said, "Did either of them say anything about an *auohe*?"

"*Auohe?*"

"You know what the word means."

"Sure, sure. Hidden place."

"Some sort of hidden place on the Big Island near the Millay ranch."

"I doan hear nothing like that."

"What about mention of the ranch or the Kona Coast?"

Headshake.

That was all Quincannon could or would get out of him. He stepped back, folded over the tail of his jacket to conceal the Navy again. Gomez let out a breath, then produced a dirty cloth that might once have been a handkerchief and smeared his face free of sweat.

"You some kine bad fella," he said then, not without a grudging measure of admiration. "What you gonna do to Vereen when you find him?"

"Mayhap the same thing I'll do to you if you tell anybody we had this little talk."

"I doan tell nobody. Not me."

"A wise decision."

"Poor Justo," Gomez said mournfully. The little half-caste had decided to feel sorry for himself. "Got all kine *pilikia nui*. Wife, four children, police, now bad kine fella like you."

Quincannon had nothing to say to that. Without turning his back to poor Justo, he took himself out into the breathless afternoon.

11

SABINA

She had most of the day to herself. Lyman had gone to his office at J. D. Spreckels and Brothers, Margaret to the school where she taught Hawaiian history, and both Kaipo and Alika had their household duties to attend to. Sabina would have welcomed the solitude under other circumstances. As it was, with John off on his grim mission, she was too restless to remain in the guesthouse awaiting his return.

In spite of her faith in his ability to keep himself from harm, a worm of worry was again at work in her—a niggling little worm that seemed to have been born when she finally admitted to herself that she was in love with him, and that plagued her whenever he was away on potentially dangerous business. Perhaps it was because she had had no such concerns about Stephen, whom she had loved with all her heart and whose sudden death had left her devastated. But Stephen had been young, as reckless as John but much less experienced, and the blind faith she had had in him was a product of her own youth and inexperience.

It was pointless to compare the two men, or her feelings for them. Her love for Stephen had been all-consuming; her love for John, the slow-developing kind of a mature woman for an equally mature man, was less intense but in a sense the bond was even stronger. In time she had been able to overcome the loss of her first love; she was not at all sure she could overcome a loss of her second and last. Hence the little worm of worry.

She went for a short stroll along Kalakaua Avenue and two short side streets. The sultry *kona* heat was less enervating today; she must be starting to become acclimatized to it. Still, she fervently hoped it would end soon. The balmy trade winds Twain and Stevenson had so highly praised would be a welcome blessing for at least a portion of their time here.

Most of the homes she passed were similar in architectural style to the Pritchards', but here and there were an odd assortment of others. One was a modified Cape Cod with a pitched gabled roof, probably by one of the New England whalers who had plied these islands in the early years of the century. Another was what Margaret would later identify as a *hale pili*—a traditional Hawaiian home built of native woods and covered with grass.

The oddest of all was the Pettibone abode. Viewed from the front, it was definitely Queen Anne in design, complete with gables and decorative shingles. No apparent modifications such as a lanai had been added. With few tropical plantings surrounding it, the house had a queer, anomalous aspect, as of something displaced in time and space. Even the carriage lean-to and stable on its far side were American in design. A Chinese groundskeeper, busily removing storm debris from the grass, also might have been transplanted from one of San Francisco's better neighborhoods.

Margaret had told her some of the house's curious history. Gordon Pettibone had hired a San Francisco architect and a six-man construction crew who specialized in building Queen Anne homes, and paid their passage to Honolulu along with all the necessary timbers and other components. The crew, with the aid of Chinese laborers—Pettibone refused to hire native Hawaiians for the task— had built the house to specifications on the property here. It must have cost him a pretty penny to have his obsessive (John would have called it "crackbrain") desire satisfied. Fortunately there was no sign of either the eccentric Mr. Pettibone or his unpleasant nephew on the grounds when she passed.

Shortly after Sabina returned to the guesthouse, Kaipo brought a light lunch of steamed butterfish wrapped in taro leaves, rice, and fruit. At first the meal didn't strike Sabina as particularly appealing, but she found that she was hungrier than she thought and the food so good she ate it all. Drowsiness overtook her not long after she finished.

She napped for nearly two hours, awoke feeling damp and sticky, and since John still hadn't returned, she donned her bathing costume and walked down to the beach. It was mostly deserted, the surf less settled than it had been the day before, the rollers breaking over the sand in restless mutters. Not really swimmable, she decided. She went in just far enough to immerse her body, then sat beneath one of the palms to dry before trekking back.

She had finished sluicing off salt residue with fresh water from the rain barrel and was dressing when John finally arrived at the guesthouse.

As soon as she saw him she knew that the day had not gone well for him. If he had succeeded in capturing the two grifters, he would have had a satisfied, even jaunty mien in spite of the heat. As it was, he looked bedraggled, vexed, his jaw set in a grimly determined way.

"What happened?" she asked. "Didn't Fenner have Vereen and Nagle located after all?"

"He had them located well enough. They've been occupying a bungalow on Punchbowl Hill the past week."

"But you didn't find them there?"

"I found one. Nagle. Dead."

"Dead? How?"

"Morphine overdose. Possibly accidental, possibly not."

"And Vereen?"

"Gone, bag and baggage."

"Gone where, do you know?"

"The Big Island," he said. "Evidently to meet with the new mark they'd set up, a man named Millay." He went on to explain who Millay was, and that the cattleman had apparently made the acquaintance of the two thieves while on a visit to San Francisco.

"Another stock swindle?" Sabina asked.

"Doesn't appear to be, this time." John removed his jacket, took a folded piece of paper from the inside pocket, and handed it to her. "Something to do with a clock or cloak, apparently. And with this."

She studied the crudely drawn map he handed her, while he sat on one of the beds and began to strip off his sweat-sodden shirt. "A drawing of one of the islands?"

"Yes. The one they call the Big Island."

"Where did you find it?"

"Sewn into the lining of Nagle's coat. Perhaps drawn by him, perhaps not. The key word is '*auohe*'—hidden place. The other words are the names of villages on the Kona Coast."

"What sort of hidden place?"

"That remains to be learned."

"Where does the clock or cloak fit in?"

"Good question." John recounted his conversation with the man named Gomez. "He claimed he didn't know which it was."

"The truth?"

"I think so. Whichever it is, it has to be something or part of something of great value."

"I can't imagine any kind of clock or cloak being worth enough to bring those two all the way here to Hawaii. Can you?"

"No," he said darkly. "But I'll find out."

She waited until he washed his hands and face at the basin and put on a clean shirt from the wardrobe trunk, then said as she returned the map, "Naturally you intend to go after Vereen."

"Naturally. I've already booked passage to the Big Island on an inter-island steamer."

"Leaving when?"

"Early tomorrow morning."

Sabina repressed a sigh. "Sure to be a lengthy trip. Several days if not longer."

"No doubt. And before you suggest it, my love, the answer is no, you cannot accompany me. Too dangerous, too much of a hardship. The Millay ranch is more than thirty miles from the nearest port of entry, over what promises to be rough terrain and primitive roads."

"I wasn't going to suggest going with you."

"Weren't you? You had that look in your eye."

"What look?"

"The same one as in Sacramento last fall, when you insisted on joining the hunt for the head of the gold-stealing ring."

"An entirely different situation," Sabina said. "You misinterpreted what I'm thinking, John."

"And what is that?"

"For one thing, that you'll need clothing, incidentals. How will you carry them? All we brought with us are these trunks."

"I hadn't thought of that." No, of course he hadn't; one of his minor faults was a tendency to overlook practical matters in times of stress. "The Pritchards must have a carpetbag I can borrow."

"Yes, but they may not want to lend it to you."

"What do you mean?"

"That is the other thing on my mind—the Pritchards. We have to tell them exactly what sort of consultants we are and the primary reason why you're here. As soon as possible."

"That isn't necessary—"

"Yes, it is, for more than one reason."

"What reasons?"

"Use your head, John. You can't just disappear for days, leaving me behind, without a credible explanation. And for all we know Margaret and Lyman may not want me to remain as their guest until you return."

"Why wouldn't they want you to remain here?"

"We haven't been completely honest with them, have we? They're respected members of the community; they may not want to become involved, even peripherally, with criminals, one of whom may have been murdered by his partner."

John started to tug at his damaged ear, fluffed his beard instead. "I see what you mean," he admitted. "But they can't be told about Nagle."

"Not that, no. Nor of Vereen's identity or any other particulars of the investigation."

"All right, then. But suppose they don't want you to remain here? What will you do?"

"Move," Sabina said. "There must be a hotel that has an accommodation available for a new guest."

The statement produced a scowl. "I don't like the idea of that."

"Neither do I, and perhaps it won't be necessary. But if it is, we'll arrange to move right away."

"Tonight? What if a hotel room can't be found on short notice?"

"Then you may have to postpone your voyage until Wednesday. A day's hiatus won't make that much difference, will it?"

"It might."

"A bridge to be crossed if and when, in any event," Sabina said. "You do agree that our hosts must be told?"

He made grumbling noises, but he knew she was right and he put up no further argument.

The Pritchards were somewhat nonplussed but not in the least upset. Margaret, in fact, seemed intrigued by the revelation that both John and Sabina were professional detectives of long standing. Lyman, as befitted a successful business executive, was more reserved; he gave his ginger mustache several thoughtful strokes before saying, "I do wish you'd told us all this on the ship."

"It would have required more explanation than we felt comfort-able providing," Sabina said. "We seldom advertise our profession unless absolutely necessary. But we do apologize for misleading you."

John asked in his blunt fashion, "Would you have invited us to be your guests if we had revealed ourselves?"

"Well . . ."

"Of course we would have." Margaret's color was high, her chocolate-drop eyes agleam. She said to Sabina, "Detective work must be thrilling. But isn't it dangerous for a woman?"

"Hardly ever." A little white lie.

"Is there any danger from the confidence man you're after?"

"Very little," John said. "Guile is his stock-in-trade, not violence." A little white lie of his own.

"Whom has he gone to see on the Big Island?" Lyman asked. "Or do you know?"

"I know, but I would rather not give you a name or any other de-tails now. Perhaps after I have my man in custody."

"How long do you expect that will take?"

"I can't say. Possibly as long as a week, given the amount of travel involved."

Sabina said, "And I have no desire to impose further on your hos-pitality while John is gone. Perhaps it would be best if I moved to a hotel until his return—"

"Oh, no, Sabina," Margaret said, "that isn't necessary, not at all. You're perfectly welcome to stay on here. Isn't she, Lyman?"

"Yes, of course," her husband agreed without hesitation. "You're friends, not just guests. The nature of your profession doesn't change that in the slightest."

Rain fell again during the night, but it was relatively light and intermittent—not much of a storm this time. Sabina would have liked to share John's bed with him, but it was too muggy for close contact of any kind. She contented herself with the thought that he would be spared any lingering concern for her welfare while he was away. The Pritchards could not have been more understanding or accommodating; Lyman had not only loaned John the carpetbag he needed, but had arranged for Alika to drive him to the inter-island steamship dock in the morning.

She did not expect to find much pleasure in the days until his return, but the company of friendly faces would make the waiting easier than if she had to tolerate it alone.

12

QUINCANNON

The night's rain had re-choked the morning with steaming humidity. Banks of black-rimmed cumulus clouds blotted out the sun. Quincannon knew without asking either Lyman, who was on his way to his job at the Spreckels office, or Alika on the buggy ride to the inter-island steamship dock, that another *kona* storm was in the offing. He could only maintain the dismal hope that it would hold off until he had completed passage to the Big Island.

It didn't, curse the luck.

The storm struck when the little steamer *Lehua* was an hour out from Honolulu Harbor, a more intense blow than the one on Saturday night. Crackles of thunder, slashing blades of lightning, heavy rain, gusting wind combined to boil the sea and toss the ship around like a toy. Quincannon endured it as he had those two days on the *Alameda*, flat on his back with eyes shut and teeth gritted against an ebb and flow of nausea.

Thankfully this tempest blew itself out not long before the ship reached Hilo. He emerged from his cabin, shaken and wobbly, as they drew into the harbor. The offshore wind that greeted him seemed somewhat cooler, but it did nothing to improve either his physical or mental well-being. He leaned on the railing, staring at the distantly looming presence of one of the island's volcanoes,

Mauna Loa, and the small port settlement that stretched out beyond a long expanse of palm-fringed beach.

The wharf at which the steamer docked looked new, as did some of the rows of warehouses along the waterfront. Hilo's buildings and houses were a mixture of old and new, some made of stone, more of unpainted timber, more still of woven palm fronds with grass roofs. Quincannon regarded the town with a dully covetous eye. It was not a particularly inviting place, but it had one attribute that made him yearn to be disembarking here: its buildings sprawled across solid ground.

The *Lehua*'s layover was short. Most of the passengers disembarked here; a handful took their place. Cargo was quickly off-loaded and other cargo loaded on, and they were soon under way again. The ocean on the leeward side of the island was considerably calmer, permitting Quincannon to remain on deck throughout the voyage around to the Kona Coast. The brisk sea wind was refreshing; his tortured insides eased. When the ship finally drew in to Kailua, he felt more or less human again.

The village was a straggling affair of thirty or forty buildings that hugged the shore beside a protected bay. The dominant structure, he overheard one of the stewards say, was a royal palace built by Prince Kuakini, brother of Kamehameha's queen. To his jaundiced eye, it looked less like a palace than a square, three-storied New England house onto which had been grafted a long porch and a second-story balcony with ornate railings.

Quincannon noted all of this abstractedly as he off-loaded himself and his borrowed carpetbag, first onto the slender dock and then onto blessed terra firma. Local color, even the exotic variety he had encountered so far in these islands, was of little interest to him at the best of times. And these were not the best of times.

He trudged to a small, single-story hotel that the steward had pointed out to him. The weather was almost as hot and sultry here as it had been in Honolulu, the sky heavy with more of the black-edged cumulus clouds. There was sure to be another blasted storm by nightfall.

The hotel accommodations were Spartan but adequate. The owner, Abner Bannister, a rail-thin Englishman with a bristling salt-and-pepper mustache, proudly proclaimed himself the descendant of one of the missionaries who had helped Prince Kuakini design his royal home in 1837. Quincannon allowed as how he was there on a business matter concerning Stanton Millay and an acquaintance, James Varner, who had arrived together on Sunday. Had Bannister seen them? No, the innkeeper said. Millay preferred other lodgings when he spent a night in Kailua.

"How far is the Millay ranch from here?" Quincannon asked.

"About thirty miles, as the crow flies."

"How would he and Varner have traveled to it? By boat?"

The hotel owner shook his head. "The only boats in Kailua are fisherman's outriggers. There are no passenger craft to Puako, the nearest village on that section of the coast. Of course, if one of the cattle ships from Hilo was due in, it could take you to Kawaihae farther north. They anchor offshore there when ranchers drive their herds to the beach for shipment to the other islands. The cattle are lashed to the outside of small boats and ferried out to the main ship where they're belly-hoisted aboard—"

"The two of them went by road, then," Quincannon interrupted. "There is one to that section of the coast, I trust?"

"Oh, yes. The up-island road goes all the way to Waimea."

"Where can I rent a horse?"

Bannister laughed. "There are no horses for hire in Kailua. The *lios* in this district have either been domesticated for use on the ranches and plantations, or roam wild."

"How do people make the trip, then? How did Millay and Varner?"

"By horse and buggy, in their case. Millay boards his equipage at the livery here when he's away. Your method of transportation will have to be by rented wagon and Kona nightingale."

"What, pray tell, is a Kona nightingale?"

"A native breed of donkey. Durable and sturdy creatures, for the most part quite dependable when domesticated."

Donkeys! No boats, no horses, naught but wagons and asses! What other handicaps did these island gardens of delight hold in store?

Bannister sent one of his Hawaiian employees to make transportation arrangements for the following morning, saving Quincannon at least that disagreeable task. After a roast pork supper, palatable save for that strange paste-like inedible side dish called *poi*, the two men retired to the hotel parlor to smoke their pipes. If there were any other guests, they had not made themselves visible in the dining room or elsewhere on the premises.

Bannister was the loquacious type, and again willing to share confidences. He was also, it developed, something of a local historian. Quincannon asked him about the Millay ranch, stating that he knew relatively little of its operation or of the family; his business with the Millays and James Varner, he said, was of a highly sensitive and private nature. The hotel owner accepted this without question.

"It's one of the larger ranches in South Kohala," Bannister said. "Several thousand acres extending from the lower slopes of Mauna Kea to the sea. And several thousand head of cattle. Grace and Stanton's father, Gregory Millay, was deeded the land by Queen Kapiʻolani at the behest of John Parker, the owner of the largest cattle ranch on the island. Parker was an intimate of King Kamehameha and the first to domesticate the wild herds of longhorns brought to the island in 1793, and Gregory Millay was one of his employees. Hawaiian longhorns are small and wiry, you know, not like the Texas variety . . ."

Quincannon cut this short by saying, "I understand Grace Millay is the guiding force behind the ranch today."

"Ever since Gregory's death eight years ago, yes. With the help of a dozen or so *paniolos* and her *luna*, Sam Opaka."

"*Paniolos? Luna?*"

"*Paniolos* are Hawaiian cowboys. '*Luna*' means 'ranch foreman.' Rough sort, Opaka, half-caste. There are rumors, but I for one pay no attention to them. Gossip is a tool of the devil."

Yes, and of a detective on the hunt. "Rumors about Grace Millay and Sam Opaka, do you mean?"

"Sadly, yes. Neither is married and they are often seen together, and so the inevitable conclusions are drawn. Grace Millay is a handsome woman. But, ah, willful and tenacious, if you know what I mean."

"That I do." If any man understood forceful women, it was John Frederick Quincannon. The description was one he himself might have used to describe Sabina, though in a complimentary fashion in her case. "And her brother? He has no objection to her running the ranch?"

"Evidently not. He's younger than she by some five years, just twenty-seven, and prefers the buying and selling end of the cattle business. Or so he claims."

"I've been told he often travels to Honolulu, and occasionally to San Francisco, and is known as quite a sport."

"Yes, well, he has that reputation." Bannister smiled wryly. "Gregory Millay had reason to be proud of at least one of his offspring."

Meaning his daughter, Quincannon surmised. "I take it you don't particularly care for Stanton Millay."

The innkeeper countered the question by asking one of his own. "How well do you know the lad?"

"Not at all—we've never met. My business is primarily with James Varner. You won't give offense by confiding your honest opinion, Mr. Bannister. I would like to know what to expect of Mr. Millay."

"Well . . . just between us?"

Quincannon raised a solemn hand. "You have my word as a gentleman that anything you say will not be repeated."

"Well and good, then," Bannister said. "My opinion is that Mr. Millay is half the man his father was—an arrogant blowhard who never outgrew his adolescence."

"The sort who would rather play than work."

"Yes."

"Weak-willed, easily manipulated, would you say?"

Bannister wouldn't say. His answer was an eloquent shrug.

"This may seem an odd question," Quincannon said then, "but I have my reasons for asking it. Do you know of any spot on that part of the coast that might be referred to as '*auohe*'?"

"Hidden place? Well, let me think." Bannister's pipe had gone out; he relit it, puffed reflectively for several seconds. "There isn't much on that part of the coast except volcanic rock, black sand beaches, and a *kiawe* forest to the east. But there are numerous caves and lava tubes, some quite large and reputed to extend for miles. Is that what you mean?"

"Possibly. What exactly is a lava tube?"

"Just what the name implies. Tubes formed centuries ago when molten flows from Mauna Kea cooled and hardened as they neared the sea and new flows tunneled through. Legend has it that there are undiscovered burial chambers in tubes along the Kohala Coast."

"Burial chambers?"

"It was the custom of the ancient kings and those of royal blood to have their clothing and other possessions interred with their remains, after the fashion of the Egyptians. The locations were kept secret for privacy reasons. . . ." Bannister paused. "Ah, that reminds me. Just south of the Millay ranch road, near Waimae Point, there is an inlet where an old *heiau* once stood. I suppose it might be considered a hidden place."

"And what is a *heiau*?"

"A Polynesian temple. After a volcanic eruption destroyed part of the low cliffs there long ago, a *kahunapule*—a high priest—ordered a temple built on the site. Grass huts that housed various wooden idols, stone altar platforms where sacrifices were offered to the gods. The early missionaries had the huts and idols burned. No one goes to the ruins."

"No? Why is that?"

"Natives are superstitious," Bannister said, "and *heiaus* were considered taboo—still are, to some extent. The ruins can also be dangerous at high tide. The rocks are unstable and there is a rather large *puka* in the ledge there. Blowhole, that is."

Quincannon let the conversation lapse. No matter now whether or not the *heiau* was the hidden place referred to on the map. Vereen would reveal the answer, one way or another.

13

SABINA

She could not seem to sleep beyond a series of fitful dozes.

It wasn't the heat or the humidity, or the fact that, except for the faint distant sound of the surf, the night had a preternatural stillness. It was that she was alone in the guesthouse. After Stephen's death she had adapted well enough to solitary living and to sleeping alone, even learned to cherish solitude; self-reliance had made her a stronger woman. Nor had she had any trouble sleeping alone during John's infrequent absences since their marriage. But here in Hawaii, in a strange environment three thousand miles from home, she couldn't help feeling a restless sense of displacement, of being at loose ends now that he was away.

Lying awake, she wished she had insisted on going with him to the Big Island. Sharing whatever hardships he might endure over there would have been preferable to the hardship of passively waiting. Margaret had graciously offered to show her the local attractions— they had spent most of this day on a buggy trip to Diamond Head, the views from the top of which were breathtaking—and she was good company if a little too inquisitive about Sabina's investigative experiences. So the days would be tolerable enough until John's return. It was the nights, if this one was an indication, that would be the hardest to bear.

The inability to do more than doze drove her out of bed finally, out onto the screened porch. There had been no rain tonight, nor was there any threat of it in the offing. The moon was up, nearly full, bright when not obscured by a thin scud of clouds. Perhaps a walk on the beach would tire her enough so she could sleep.

She dressed in a skirt and blouse, slipped her bare feet into beach sandals, tied a long scarf around her head and neck, and went outside. The lack of even a breath of ocean breeze made the night's stillness acute, and the mingled scents of tropical flowers were almost cloyingly sweet. The whiteness of intermittent moonlight made it easy enough for her to traverse the crushed-shell path that led down to the beach. Mosquitoes and other night bugs thrummed around her on the way, but they were not bothersome enough to change her mind about continuing.

When she reached the gate, she could see lights in every direction—a winking yellow beacon high atop the massive shape of Diamond Head, winking lanterns out beyond the reef that marked the presence of native fishing boats, a broad sweep of shore and ship lights in the harbor three miles away, the glow of the arcs that lined the city streets. The sight, not unlike that of the San Francisco bay front as seen from Nob Hill or Telegraph Hill on a clear night, gave birth to a faint feeling of homesickness. As much as she liked Hawaii and the Pritchards, the visit here had not lived up to her expectations thus far.

She stepped through the gate, walked southward along the surf line. There was no one else on the beach at this hour—3:00 A.M.? 4:00? It was as if she were alone on a desert isle, a feeling that was not unpleasant. Sabina Crusoe, she thought, and smiled.

She had not walked far, a hundred rods or so, when she came upon what she thought at first was a large round rock in the sand. But as she neared it, it moved. The partial appearance of a dark scaly head froze her to a standstill. Then the head retreated and the shape was motionless again, and she realized what it was. A turtle, a harmless giant sea turtle that had crawled up onto the beach to sleep. She chuckled to herself, detoured around the creature, and made her way back the way she'd come.

The Pettibone house had been completely dark when she started out; now a light shone in a pair of adjacent windows in a ground-floor room facing the sea. Someone there who wasn't able to sleep either, she thought. But maybe she could now; she felt tired enough after the stroll. She stepped through the gate, went up through the garden.

She was almost to the guesthouse porch when an explosive report broke the quiet.

The noise brought her to another standstill, the hairs on the back of her scalp prickling. No mistaking it for anything other than a gunshot; she had heard enough pistols fired to recognize it. Yes, and the shot had to have come from a large-caliber weapon for the sound to have carried on the still night air.

There was no second report; the silence resettled. Instinct and curiosity sent her past the poinciana tree to the boundary fence, to where she had a mostly unobstructed view of the Pettibone house. At her first look she saw nothing but a pale spill of electric light from one of the rear windows. Seconds later, a puffball cloud obscured the moon, throwing a blanket of darkness over the house and grounds.

Sabina thought she saw movement then, a vague shadow shape close to the back wall. She strained forward, squinting. Movement again? She couldn't be sure; her eyes might have been playing tricks on her. And she saw nothing more. The shadow shape, if it had been there at all, had vanished.

Other lights bloomed in the house, upstairs first and then downstairs. Alarmed voices filtered out, at least two, both loud enough for her to hear but not for the words to be distinguishable. Shouts, followed by a series of hollow poundings as of fists beating against wood. More shouts, louder, one of them carrying a word that might have been "Uncle!" And then more noises, these unidentifiable.

The moon reappeared, bathing the house in a talcumy whiteness.

Sabina stepped closer to the fence. It was of bamboo and some two feet in height, little more than a boundary marker.

Don't become involved!

She paid no heed to the inner warning. She had never backed away from a crisis situation no matter how much personal peril it might entail; was professionally and constitutionally incapable of it. Well trained, inquisitive, and probably too fearless for her own good. If someone had been harmed in the Pettibone house, there might be aid she could render. She raised her skirts, climbed over the low fence, and crossed at an angle toward the rear of the house.

At first she made haste, but the ground was uneven in spots, the turf littered with small obstacles of storm debris. The toe of her sandal caught on something, nearly tripped her, and caused her to slow her pace. When she reached the rear corner, she paused before stepping cautiously around it. The light came through the near window, she saw then; the one adjacent was shuttered. Not quite into the light, she craned her head forward until she could look through the window past parted drapes.

Her view of the chandelier-lit room beyond was limited, but she saw enough to confirm that a tragedy had taken place there. There were four people in the room, all of them clad in what appeared to be hastily donned robes. Philip Oakes and a middle-aged Chinese man were bent over a motionless form lying prone on the floor, one arm outflung as if reaching for the handgun a short distance away; the secretary, Earlene Thurmond, hovered behind them. The fallen man's face was turned away, but his dust-gray hair and liver-spotted scalp left no doubt that he was Gordon Pettibone.

The Chinese man raised his head, and Sabina quickly withdrew. She backed around the corner, turned from the house. The moonlight was still bright as she began picking her way back across the grass.

She was halfway to the boundary fence when the side porch door flew open and Philip Oakes came hurrying out.

He couldn't miss seeing her, and didn't. He called, "Who is it? Who goes there?"

Uh-oh—caught. Sabina halted. Nothing to do now but stand her ground and make the best of it.

Oakes ran up to her, the tails of his flowered robe flapping around him. "Cheng thought he saw someone out here . . . oh, it's you, Mrs. Quincannon. What are you doing here?"

"I couldn't sleep and went for a walk on the beach. I was on my way back when I heard what sounded like a pistol shot. Other noises, too. I know I shouldn't have trespassed, but—"

He waved that away. "Never mind. Never mind. It was a pistol shot you heard."

"What happened?"

"My uncle shot himself."

"Oh, I'm so sorry. Is he badly hurt?"

"He's dead. Dead." Oakes did not sound distraught, or even particularly upset. His only emotional reaction appeared to be a mild agitation. "It was an accident. Locked himself in the study, fiddled with that pistol of his, and it went off and blew a hole in his chest. Dead as a doornail."

Sabina couldn't help asking, "Was he in the habit of doing that?"

"Doing what?"

"Locking himself in his study at this hour with a loaded pistol."

"I don't know. He might have been, he had queer habits. Queer habits." Oakes shook his head as if to refocus his thoughts. "The police," he said then, "I have to telephone for the police. You'll inform the Pritchards, will you? They'll want to know of the accident. *Accident,*" he repeated, stressing the word this time.

"Yes, of course I will."

They went in separate directions, Oakes back to the side porch and Sabina across the grass and over the fence near the guesthouse. Lights shone in two of the upstairs windows in the main house; Lyman and Margaret, Alika and Kaipo must have been awakened by the noises. That made Sabina's task a little easier. She hadn't relished the choice of either waking the household herself at this hour or waiting until dawn to honor her promise.

It was Lyman who opened the front door in answer to her ring. His eyes expressed surprise that she was fully dressed at this hour, but she forestalled comment by saying she had urgent news. He ushered her into the living room, where Margaret joined them. The Pritchards naturally expressed shock at the news of Gordon Pettibone's sudden demise, and not a little puzzlement at the circumstances.

"I don't understand how such a terrible thing could happen," Margaret said. One of her ash-blond curls had come unpinned and drooped down over her forehead; absently she brushed it back into place. Her eyes were sad as well as bemused.

"Mr. Oakes seems convinced it was an accident." Overly convinced for some reason—a thought Sabina kept to herself.

"Gordon was certainly eccentric," Lyman said, "but I can't imagine him sitting in his study cleaning or handling a pistol in the middle of the night."

"Did he collect firearms?"

"I don't believe so. We've been to his home a few times and I never saw any."

Margaret said, "It must have been an accident. I can't imagine him taking his own life. Or anyone in the household wanting to . . . well . . . harm him."

Sabina hadn't mentioned the vague shadow shape; she still was not sure it had been anything other than a figment of her imagination. But the memory of it, real or not, prompted her to ask, "Are you aware of any enemies Mr. Pettibone might have had?"

Lyman finger-combed his mustache, shook his head. "Not everyone in the business community approved of his methods, but enemies? No, not to my knowledge."

"Good relations with the others in the household?"

The Pritchards exchanged glances. Again it was Lyman who answered. "As far as we know. Gordon and Philip had their disagreements, as I expect you noticed Saturday evening, but there seemed to be no real hostility between them."

Margaret said impulsively, "I doubt that Cheng and Miss Thurmond cared for him. He treated them as if they were slaves."

That brought a reproof from her husband. "You mustn't speak ill of the dead, my dear. It hardly matters now what faults Gordon may have had."

It did, Sabina thought, if his death had been neither accidental nor willful . . . that shadow shape again. But there was no point in allowing herself to pursue the possibility of foul play. Gordon Pettibone's death was a matter for the police to deal with, and none of her business in any case.

"Yes, you're right, I'm sorry," Margaret said to Lyman. Then, "I wonder if there is anything we can do for Philip and Miss Thurmond."

"You mean now? No. We would only be in the way when the police arrive. Tomorrow is soon enough to offer condolences." He stifled a yawn, rose to his feet. "What we need to do now is go back to bed."

"There'll be no more sleep for me tonight."

"There must be for me—I have to be in the office at nine. That may sound callous," he added for Sabina's benefit, "but life goes on no matter how close to home tragedy strikes."

A cliché, but a valid one. For the Pritchards, if not so aptly for Sabina. This was not her home and the tragedy next door was hers only by proximity and random happenstance. She would have to remain a guest of the Pritchards until John returned, an even less pleasant prospect now. Then they would move into a hotel in Honolulu proper, or perhaps simply book passage on the first available steamship bound for San Francisco.

Yet she lay wide-awake in the guesthouse bed, unable even to doze. Tonight's tragedy might have only peripherally affected her, but she could not get what she had ear- and eye-witnessed out of her mind. The vague shadow shape hovered like a chimera.

She listened to the muted night sounds, enduring the muggy, overheated air. *Kona* weather. The words of the tubby little man on the deck of the steamer Saturday morning came back to her: *The Polynesians believed that* kona *weather is "dying weather."*

Prophetic for Nevada Ned Nagle.

And now for Gordon Pettibone.

14

SABINA

Later that day she had two visitors, the first not unexpected, the second whose purpose was something of a surprise.

Margaret came to fetch her when the first caller arrived at the main house midmorning. Emil Jacobsen, captain of detectives, Honolulu Police. He unfolded himself from a chair in the living room when they entered—a tall, spare man with a long, narrow face and jaw, and a skullcap of iron-gray hair, clad not in a uniform but a tan business suit, white shirt, and plum-colored bow tie. Margaret plainly would have liked to remain while he spoke with Sabina, but propriety won out over curiosity and she silently withdrew.

The captain introduced himself, favoring Sabina with a courtly bow and a solemn smile as he did so. His manner was not quite deferential. And expressive, she thought, of more than an ordinary amount of professional interest.

When they were seated he said, "As I'm sure you've surmised, I asked to speak with you regarding the death of Mr. Gordon Pettibone."

"Yes, but there is really nothing I can tell you that I didn't tell Mr. Oakes last night. Other than I regret having given in to impulse and trespassed on the Pettibone property."

"Understandable in the circumstances. Would you mind repeating exactly what you saw and heard?"

"Not at all," she said, and did so. Including mention of the shadow shape. It was seldom wise to withhold anything from the police, John's views about the efficacy of the law notwithstanding, and would have been downright foolish to do so in a foreign land.

Captain Jacobsen was not stirred. "So you can't be certain that you actually saw such movements?"

"No, I can't."

"You had yet to step over onto the Pettibone property at the time?"

"That's correct. The angle of view from where I stood was oblique and the light from the window not bright."

"An optical illusion," he said, and punctuated the statement with a positive nod. "The circumstances of Mr. Pettibone's death are such that he could have died in only one of two ways, by accident or by his own hand."

"The circumstances?"

"He was alone in his study, the door and both windows locked. The door had to be broken down—the noises you heard following the shot."

"Yes, I thought as much," Sabina said. "May I ask what conclusion you've reached?"

He studied her for a few seconds, as if trying to decide how candid he should be. Then, "I am satisfied that Mr. Pettibone took his own life, though it's up to the coroner to make the final determination."

That was not the verdict she had expected. "Mr. Oakes seemed adamant that the shooting was accidental."

"Very adamant, understandably so, but incorrect. Mr. Pettibone kept his pistol in his bedroom—he deliberately took it into the study last night. There were no cleaning supplies in the study, so that couldn't have been his purpose. Everything points to suicide."

"Wasn't the fatal wound in his chest? Mr. Oakes said it was."

"It was, yes."

"Don't those who commit suicide by firearm usually shoot themselves in the head?"

"Not always. A bullet in the heart is not uncommon."

"Did Mr. Pettibone leave a suicide note?"

"No, but that is also not uncommon. And his dying words are surely meaningless."

"Dying words?"

"He was still alive when Mr. Oakes and the houseman broke in. He spoke three words before he died. 'Pick up sticks.'"

Sabina repeated the phrase. "Is it certain that those are the words he spoke?"

Captain Jacobsen raised and lowered his long jaw affirmatively. "Mr. Oakes, the houseman, and Mr. Pettibone's secretary all heard them."

"Do any of them have an idea of what he meant?"

"No," he said. "Evidently the words had no specific meaning— the delusional rambling of a dying man *in extremis*."

Perhaps, but it seemed a strange phrase for a man such as Gordon Pettibone to have uttered at any time, much less with his last breath. For no particular reason it put Sabina in mind of the old nursery rhyme: One, two, buckle my shoe. Three, four, knock on the door. Five, six, pick up sticks. Very strange, indeed.

The captain was scrutinizing her again. His smile, now, had an ironic edge. "You're very inquisitive, Mrs. Quincannon. A result of your profession, no doubt. Mrs. Pritchard told me that you and your husband operate a detective agency in San Francisco."

Drat! Margaret meant well, but Sabina's accounts of her experiences had resulted in a touch of idolization that had loosened her hostess's tongue. That explained the captain's added professional interest.

He said, "I don't believe I've heard of a woman detective in the private sector. You must be unique in the profession."

The one thing that irritated Sabina almost as much as having men criticize or scoff at her chosen livelihood was having them consider her "unique," as if she were a freak of nature instead of an emancipated woman toiling willfully and successfully in a man's game. Captain Jacobsen, at least, showed no disrespect. In fact, he seemed mildly intrigued.

She curbed her annoyance. "Not at all," she said. "I was employed and trained by the Pinkerton Agency, as several other women have been, before I entered into partnership with Mr. Quincannon. Nearly a dozen years' experience, all told."

"Commendable," he said, and seemed to mean it. "Mrs. Pritchard sang your praises with what I have no doubt is complete justification. But you are in Honolulu on vacation?"

"I am, yes."

"Your husband has business here and on the Big Island, I understand."

Margaret again, not that the source mattered. An explanation of John's absence would have had to be tendered in any case. But not a full explanation, even if one were demanded; he would provide the details of his pursuit of Lonesome Jack Vereen and the late Nevada Ned Nagle if and when he delivered Vereen to the local authorities.

"He does," Sabina said, "a private matter on behalf of a client who demands discretion. I'm sure you understand."

"I do, unless it in any way breaks or circumvents Hawaiian law." Time for a little white lie. "I assure you that it doesn't."

Captain Jacobsen accepted that and did not press her further. He rose, said it had been a pleasure meeting her, bowed again, and took his leave.

After he was gone, Sabina briefly, gently, and mildly remonstrated with Margaret, asking that she please not reveal her and John's profession to anyone else. Margaret apologized profusely, and that settled the matter.

Sabina's second visitor arrived unannounced at the guesthouse shortly past noon. She had just finished partaking of a light lunch brought by Kaipo and was perusing an article in the current issue of the *Honolulu Evening Bulletin* criticizing the burgeoning influx of American warships and military personnel when the knock came on the screen door. She opened it, and there stood Philip Oakes.

"I hope I'm not intruding, Mrs. Quincannon," he said. "I'd like to speak to you. May I come in?"

"Speak to me about what, Mr. Oakes?"

"My uncle's death. *May* I come in?"

There was none of Saturday evening's flirtatiousness in the way he looked at her, nor was he nattily well groomed or his manner urbane, so it was not a foolishly ill-timed attempt at seduction that had brought him. He seemed more upset today than he had been when she'd spoken to him last night. His voice and eyes were both beseeching.

She allowed him inside. He waited until she had reseated herself at the rattan table, then occupied the second chair and mopped his face with an embroidered silk handkerchief. In the close confines of the porch she detected the odor of whiskey on his breath, but it was not strong and he was nowhere near intoxicated. A large drink or two to settle his nerves, at a guess.

"I've come to ask your help," he said.

"My help? To do what?"

"Prove that my uncle's death was an accident. An *accident*. You're a detective, aren't you? Captain Jacobsen told me you were after he spoke with you."

Oh, Lord. The police detective had been no more circumspect than Margaret had in keeping her profession confidential. "Yes," she admitted, "I am. In San Francisco."

"There is nothing to stop you from practicing your trade here, is there? Detective business is why your husband went to the Big Island, isn't it?"

Sabina swallowed a sigh. "The captain seems convinced your uncle died by his own hand."

"Jacobsen is wrong. My uncle would never have committed suicide. Never."

"You're sure of that?"

"Positive. He was too fond of himself, had too much to live for. Great Orient Import-Export, his position with the Reform Party and the annexation. Yes, and finishing the book on ancient Chinese history he was writing. I told Jacobsen all of this but he wouldn't listen, just wouldn't listen. His investigation was cursory, he made up his mind in a hurry. The man is an incompetent blockhead."

"An incompetent blockhead doesn't become a captain of detectives," Sabina said.

"He does if he was given his position for political reasons. Jacobsen was. He must have been."

"What makes you think I am any more competent than he? How do you expect me to prove him wrong?"

"Come with me to the house, conduct your own investigation. There must be something the police missed in my uncle's study, *something* they missed. I'll pay you. I'll pay whatever your agency charges in San Francisco."

"Payment is not an issue," Sabina said. "Why are you so desperate to prove your uncle did not take his own life?"

"Suicide is bad for business. Bad for business. A blot on the family escutcheon."

"Come now, Mr. Oakes, you're not being frank with me. There must be more to it than that."

He was silent for a few seconds, as if debating with himself. Then, "Oh, very well. The main reason is insurance."

"Insurance?"

"A life insurance policy with an American firm. Twenty thousand dollars. Twenty thousand dollars! I happen to know that I am the beneficiary."

"I see. The policy contains a nonpayment clause in the event of suicide, is that it?"

"Yes. Twenty thousand dollars is a substantial amount—all that is likely to come to me and I won't be cheated out of it. I won't be cheated."

"But surely you stand to inherit your uncle's home, his share of the import-export business . . ."

"Not the business," Oakes said. "There are ironclad agreements with the other partners . . . no, I don't stand to inherit his share. Or the house. Likely he left it to his business partners, or the Reform Party. Or his paramour."

"Paramour?"

"Miss Earlene Thurmond." His lip curled disdainfully as he spoke the name. "That is what she was, you know, in addition to her secretarial duties. His paramour."

Sabina let that pass without comment.

"No financial bequest to me, that is the point," Oakes said. "No money except the insurance. Not even a token amount in his will, he told me that. Not even a token amount."

"In that case, are you certain you're still the beneficiary of the insurance policy?"

"Certain, yes. Positive. My uncle was manipulative, autocratic, but he wasn't a complete bas . . . wasn't completely heartless. He hadn't much sense of family loyalty but he did have some. Not enough, but some."

Once more Sabina was silent. Unbidden, the lines from the old nursery rhyme again intruded on her thoughts. One, two, buckle my shoe. Three, four, knock on the door. Five, six . . .

"Pick up sticks," she said aloud.

"What? What's that?"

"Pick up sticks. Captain Jacobsen told me your uncle spoke those words before he succumbed. You haven't any idea what they mean?"

"No. He never said anything like that before. Never. Out of his head with pain. What does it matter?"

"Perhaps it doesn't." And perhaps it did.

Oakes mopped his forehead again. "Will you at least come to the house and look through the study? At least that much, Mrs. Quincannon?"

Sabina's inclination was to politely but firmly decline. She did not like Philip Oakes and she found his mercenary motives distasteful. And yet there were puzzling aspects to Gordon Pettibone's death that were not satisfactorily explained by Captain Jacobsen's conclusion of a willfully self-inflicted gunshot.

The fact that 3:00 A.M. was a curious time for a man to choose to take his own life; the gunshot wound in an unlikely location for a suicide; that inexplicable dying utterance of "pick up sticks"; and the shadow shape that might not have been imaginary after all.

Add all those together, and she knew what John would have made of the bundle. If the two apparent anomalies were nothing of the kind, and "pick up sticks" was not just nonsense but some sort of dying message, then it was possible Gordon Pettibone *hadn't* shot himself on purpose or by accident—that someone had put the bullet in his heart despite the fact that the study doors and windows had all been locked.

John, if he were here, would surely accept the investigative challenge; conundrums of this sort intrigued him. If she refused the opportunity, he would chastise her for it when he found out. And be perfectly right in doing so. She had, after all, been instrumental in solving a few conundrums herself.

"Very well, Mr. Oakes," she said. "I'll do as you ask."

15

QUINCANNON

Quincannon left Kailua shortly past dawn on Wednesday morning.

Rain had pelted down again during most of the night, but at this hour the sky above the village was clear. Banks of clouds on the horizon were not quite dark enough to be the harbingers of another storm; an intermittent offshore breeze carried no scent of ozone. The ever-present muggy stickiness suggested another blistering, if dry, day ahead.

The hired wagon was little more than a wooden cart with iron wheels, but its bed was large enough to hold a trussed prisoner on the return trip; now it contained only his borrowed carpetbag and a package of food and bottle of water provided by Abner Bannister. As for the creature in the traces, Quincannon had never seen one quite like it. A Kona nightingale was smaller than the four-legged asses he was used to, and resembled nothing so much as a leathery-skinned mouse grown to fifty times its normal size. He had eyed it skeptically on first encounter; it seemed incapable of either the stamina for a thirty-mile trip or the ability to move along at any but a retarded speed. The impression, at least in the early stages of the trek, had proved false. The animal trotted along the muddy, heavily rutted road with no evident strain and at a pace almost equal to that of a horse.

Kailua lay in lowlands dominated by vast plantations of coffee and sugarcane. The road ran on a more or less level grade through the fields, then began to skirt the edges of inland hills grayed by volcanic ash. Ancient lava flows from Mauna Kea had permanently scarred the landscape, leaving humped, blackened rocks to mark their path to the sea. The volcano loomed high and wide to the east, its snow-covered crest sheathed and mostly hidden by clouds. The Polynesians, Abner Bannister had told him, considered it *kahunu*—a bad mountain—because of the devastation caused by its eruptions.

By nine o'clock the heat had increased and lay heavily on Quincannon's head and shoulders. His sweat-encrusted Panama hat provided some protection from the harsh sunlight, and he allowed himself frequent sips from the water bottle. He stopped once to give the Kona nightingale a drink and a bait of grain, using the hat for a bowl. Otherwise the donkey trotted along without apparent need for rest.

Shortly past eleven by his stem-winder they crested a hill, from where he could see a considerable distance along the rugged coast. Huge blackened lava swaths cut through the greens and browns; some of the beaches were of black sand, an oddly unreal sight in their fringes of coconut palms. Where the road descended near one of these, he stopped again and sought shade under one of the palms in which to partake of the sandwiches and fruit Bannister had packed for him.

The day wore on. Mile after mile jolted away. He passed the small fishing villages that were noted on the map, Kawaihae and Puako, but saw no one on the road other than a lone rider on horseback—a cowhand from one of the ranches, from the look of him—and a handful of donkey carts driven by natives who regarded him with stoic interest, doubtless curious as to what had brought a large bearded stranger into their backcountry midst.

Sun flame and the moist air turned his disposition as black and bleak as the lava scars. There would come a day when he would look back on this adventure as an example of the ends to which an implacable detective would go to bring his quarry to justice. But that day was a long way off.

Mostly he rode with his mind empty, but once he thought of Sabina and wondered how she was spending her day. In much more pleasant circumstances than he was, he hoped. Seeing the sights with Margaret Pritchard, or lounging on the Waikiki beach in the shade of a coconut palm after a refreshing swim. The thought of immersion in the surf, despite the fact that it was as warm as bathwater, made him feel even hotter and he thrust it aside.

It was early afternoon when he reached the old temple, although he would not have recognized it as such if it hadn't been for a pair of landmarks given him by Bannister—a stunted *kukui* tree growing atilt between two spike-like rocks, and the arrowhead-shaped ledge jutting out into the sea. There might have been cliffs here at one time, but molten lava had flattened them down into a long, wide slope ridged and humped and strewn with huge black boulders.

From the road he could see the blowhole in the ledge's outer end, and below that a sandy beach neither black nor white but a dark gray. A strong offshore wind blew here and the sea had roughened under its lash; tidewater mixed with air boiled into the seaward end of what Bannister had described as a blowhole—a funnel-like tube on a wide flattened section beneath the ledge—and sent spray geysering a hundred feet into the air. The falling water drenched the rocks there, made them glisten like black glass.

Quincannon ground-hitched the donkey near the *kukui* tree. Nearby was an ancient trail leading down to the temple, but it was barely discernible; some exploration was required before he found it. The descent was gradual, but the sharp-edged lava rock made for poor footing and slow progress. As he neared the ledge, the roar and gurgle of the spouting blowhole was thunderous.

A flattish, inland extension of the ledge serpentined in among the overhanging rocks. There, hidden from the road, was where he found the ruins of the *heiau*.

All that remained standing were sections of the outer walls. Entry forbidden to natives by Polynesian law, Bannister had told him. Ancient superstitions meant nothing to Quincannon, or nothing to which he would admit in the light of day. He discovered a passage between two of the sections, followed it into an open expanse some fifty rods in diameter. The ground was uneven, littered with sharp rocks. Flat volcanic slabs, cracked and broken, appeared to have been arranged by hand at its rear—the old sacrificial stones. Nothing remained of the huts or idols that had once been displayed here.

He prowled the ruins for a time, finding nothing to have inspired the crude map or the cryptic word "*auohe*." There were several narrow, tight-fitting openings into the maze of rocks, one or more of which might have been man-made, but attempting to explore them with no more than a packet of lucifers was a fool's errand. He would need a lantern or a supply of candles for that chore. And exploration wouldn't be necessary if he could get his hands on Lonesome Jack Vereen without incident at the Millay ranch.

He climbed back up to the road and into the wagon, gigged the Kona nightingale into a fresh trot. It was a short distance to where the ranch road, marked by a weathered sign and a track worn smooth by countless wheels and hoofs, wound upward through a desolate landscape toward the brooding presence of the volcano.

The ascent was sharp and steady, curling through lava beds where the wagon's wheels churned up a powdery black grit that clogged Quincannon's nostrils and streaked his sweating face. Then it passed through the *kiawe* forest, a long jungly stretch in which the trees, none more than dozen feet in height, were so closely packed that their bare, thorn-laden branches had interwoven to form an impassable tangle on both sides of the road.

Once he emerged from the forest, the grasslands began. The wind that blew at this higher elevation was cooler by several degrees and carried the smell of grass and mountain instead of the sea.

Quincannon's spirits rose. The lethargy produced by the long, hot ride began to ease.

Eventually the road debouched into a small, verdant valley. The pastureland here was spotted with longhorn cattle, lean and somewhat stunted by comparison to the burly variety raised on California and Southwestern ranches. At the far end, set among a broad half circle of trees, he spied the ranch buildings. He adjusted the holstered Navy on his hip, smiling thinly in anticipation, when the Kọna nightingale clattered him into the ranch yard. The prospect of action, especially after a long trek, always had a limbering effect on his liver.

The ranch house, he saw as he drew near, was a long, low structure of native lumber with hand-squared log walls and a palm-thatch roof; its porch, open on three sides, was green-shadowed by the branches of a huge monkeypod tree. The visible windows had glass panes that caught the lowering rays of the sun and threw back a fiery dazzle. Several cattle pens and a corral constructed of thick bamboo poles stretched south of the house. Several outbuildings were also visible, among them a stable, dairy barn, and what was likely a bunkhouse for the hands.

Two Hawaiian cowboys clad in sweat-soaked shirts, chaps, and boots were working a pair of horses inside the corral, both animals small and wiry like Indian mustangs and marked with white pinto splotches. Another *paniolo* stood inside the open doors to a blacksmith's shop next to the stable, using a pair of heavy nippers on another horse's hoof. There was no sign of anyone at the main house.

Quincannon drew up at the far end of the yard, nearer the stable. The two *paniolos* in the corral stopped their work and came over to stand silently watching from the fence. The one in the smithy looked up but did not lower either the nippers or his animal's hoof as Quincannon approached him.

The cowhand was middle-aged, sinewy, with an expressionless

face sunburned to the hue of old mahogany. Quincannon stopped at a sidewise angle in the doorway so that he could see the corral and the house beyond.

"*Aloha,*" he said. This seemed to be the standard Islands greeting. "You wouldn't be the *luna,* by any chance? Sam Opaka?"

"No. You want Sam?"

"My business is with James Varner."

The name produced no reaction. The *paniolo* finished cutting away heavy cartilage, then picked up a wood rasp to smooth the edges and keep the hoof from splitting.

"James Varner," Quincannon said again, more sharply.

"Don't know him."

"Mr. Millay's friend from San Francisco. Arrived with him on Sunday."

"Mr. Millay got no *malihini* friend here."

"Tall man, slender, with a mane of silver hair."

The *paniolo* shrugged. "Never see nobody look like that."

"Are you sure?"

"Sure. Nobody with Mr. Millay when he come back Monday."

Quincannon stared at him. What was this, now? A lie or evasion, for some reason? If it was the truth, where the devil was Lonesome Jack Vereen?

16

QUINCANNON

Scowling, he asked the *paniolo,* "Is Mr. Millay here now?"

"Sure."

"Where would I find him?"

"Main house, maybe."

"And his sister?"

"Miss Grace out riding with Sam Opaka. Back pretty soon."

Quincannon left him to his chore and crossed the yard to the ranch house. It was almost tolerably cool in the shade of the monkeypod. The front door stood open behind a fly screen; he rattled his knuckles on the screen's frame. When this produced no response he used the heel of his hand to make a louder summons.

A voice from the gloom within called out thickly, "Mele! See who that is!"

Quincannon waited. After a minute or so, when no one appeared, he pounded on the frame again.

"Mele!" Then: "Dammit, who's making all that racket out there?"

"Stanton Millay?"

". . . I don't want to see anybody. Go away."

Quincannon did the opposite: he opened the screen and stepped inside. Once his eyes grew accustomed to the half-light, he saw that he was in a large room whose rough-hewn walls were decorated with tapa cloth on which were displayed notched war clubs and a pair of crossed spears with polished wood shafts and ivory barbs. An assortment of other pagan objects—carved idols, feathered fetishes, calabashes made from coconut husks—were arranged on pieces of furniture made of native lumber and on woven mats that covered the floor.

In one of three chairs a young, medium-sized man with a mop of wheat-colored hair sat slumped on his spine, a glass propped on his chest. Judging from the bleary squint he directed at Quincannon, the glass contained *okolehao* or its equivalent and had been emptied and refilled several times from the decanter on an adjacent table.

"Who in blazes are you?" he demanded.

"My name is Quincannon."

"Quincannon? Scotsman, eh? I don't know any Scotsmen. Get out of my house."

"Not until I have what I came here for."

"And just what would that be?"

"Jack Vereen."

A blank stare. "Who?"

"All right, then. James A. Varner."

That name produced a twitch that nearly upset Millay's glass. "Who?" he said again.

"Don't try my patience, Mr. Millay. You crossed the ocean from San Francisco with him and his partner, Simon Reno. Spent a night drinking and carousing with them in Honolulu last week."

"By Christ!" The exclamation startled a young Hawaiian girl, barefoot and dressed in a long flowered garment, who had just entered the room. "I don't want you any more, Mele," Millay snapped at her, and immediately she disappeared again. Then he said to Quincannon, "Casual companions, nothing more. What's your interest in them? Who the devil are you?"

Quincannon laid one of his business cards on the arm of Millay's chair. The rancher picked it up, squinted at the wording. A muscle flexed twice in his cheek, shaping his mouth into a grimace. He fortified himself with a deep draught from his glass before saying, "Detective? What's Varner and Reno done to bring a San Francisco detective all the way out here?"

"You have no idea?"

"No. I hardly know them, just a couple of businessmen I happened to meet."

"In San Francisco on your recent trip there."

"So what? What difference does that make?"

"The fact that they shared your passage back to Honolulu makes a great deal of difference."

"Why the hell should it? Listen—"

"No, you listen, Mr. Millay. Whether you know it or not, those two are not businessmen—they are thieves and swindlers."

This was no revelation to the cattleman. The muscle flexed again; his gaze shifted away from Quincannon's. Man under a severe nervous strain. "What does that have to do with me?"

"That is what I want to know," Quincannon said. "What kind of fabulous scheme did they present to you?"

"Scheme?"

"Something to do with a clock or cloak, wasn't it?"

The muscle flexed again. "You don't make any sense, man. Clock, cloak . . . mumbo jumbo. I had no business with those two. I told you . . . good-time companions, that's all."

Quincannon didn't believe him and said so.

"I don't care what you believe or don't believe," Millay said. He drank again. "Not one damn bit."

"Where is Varner now?"

"How should I know?"

"He came here with you on Monday."

"The hell he did."

"You left Honolulu with him Sunday morning."

". . . How do you know that?"

"How I know isn't important. Do you deny it?"

"No," Millay said. "We happened to take the same steamer, that's all. Last I saw of him was five minutes after we docked at Hilo. He was meeting someone there, he said."

"Did he, now? And who might that someone be?"

"He didn't confide in me. And I didn't ask. I keep my nose out of other men's business."

Quincannon had had enough of this verbal sparring. He growled, "Varner's true name is Vereen, Lonesome Jack Vereen. His fat partner's real name was Nagle, also known as Nevada Ned."

". . . What do you mean, his name *was* Nagle?"

"He's dead."

"Dead?" The cheek muscle danced this time. "How? When?"

"Three days ago of a morphine overdose. Possibly administered by Vereen before he departed."

"Why would—" Millay broke off, wagged his head in a confused way. "What's that got to do with me?"

"That is what I intend to find out."

"Does Varner . . . Vereen know you're after him?"

"If he doesn't," Quincannon said, "he soon will. I've come almost three thousand miles to take him prisoner and I won't leave until I do. If you're hiding him on this ranch, you're guilty of aiding and abetting a dangerous fugitive."

"Hiding him? Why would I do that?"

"Why, indeed."

"Well, I'm not hiding him. Dammit, he was never here!"

"You had better not be lying to me, Mr. Millay."

In a convulsive movement the rancher drained his glass, slammed it down on a side table hard enough to knock it over, and shoved onto his feet. "I've heard enough about matters that don't concern me. And I don't like to be threatened." The bluster was still in his thickened voice, but underlying it now was a current of fear. "Either you rattle your hocks out of here or I'll throw you out."

Quincannon's answer to that was a feral grin. In the tense moment that followed, there was the sudden pound of boots on the porch outside. Two pairs, one heavy, one light. A woman's voice called "Stan? Are you in here?" just before the screen door clattered open.

Quincannon moved a few paces to one side as the newcomers entered the room. The woman, in the lead, was an older, slimmer version of Millay—fair-skinned, her sun-bleached hair tucked inside a cowboy hat decorated with a hibiscus band. The hard-eyed man behind her was native-dark, bulky, dressed as she was in rough range garb. Grace Millay and Sam Opaka.

The woman glanced at Quincannon, said to her brother, "Keole told me we have company. Who is this man?"

"His name's Quincannon," Millay said. He seemed calmer now that reinforcements had arrived, but no less defensive or truculent. And the undercurrent of fear was still present in his voice. "Detective from San Francisco. He thinks we're harboring one of a pair of swells I met on my trip, supposed to be a confidence man."

"Jack Vereen," Quincannon said, "alias James A. Varner."

"I told him I haven't seen the man since Sunday in Hilo but he doesn't believe me." To Quincannon he said, "This is my sister, Grace. And our *luna*, Sam Opaka. Go ahead, ask them if Varner's here or been here."

"My brother is telling the truth," Grace Millay said. Opaka said nothing, but his eyes, black and hard as volcanic rock, never left Quincannon's face. "There is no one on this ranch named Varner or Vereen. Nor has there ever been, so far as I know."

"That remains to be seen."

"What makes you think this man came here?"

Quincannon said cannily, "The *auohe*, among other things."

"*Auohe*? What *auohe*?" She sounded genuinely puzzled.

"On the coast near here."

"I have no idea what you're referring to. Sam? Do you?"

Opaka gave a short, sharp headshake.

"Neither do I," Millay snapped. He had picked up the decanter from the table and was about to replenish his glass. "By God, this has gone far enough. Talking nonsense, implying we're liars—I won't stand for it!"

His sister said warningly, "Be quiet, Stan."

"Why should I? I don't want anything more to do with this damn flycop. I think we ought to kick his *okole* off our land. Sam and me, right now."

"I told you to be quiet. And put that decanter down. You've had enough to drink."

"The hell I have."

"More than enough." She nodded to Opaka. "Sam."

The *luna* moved for the first time. He caught hold of Millay's arm with one hand, the decanter with the other. He said softly, "Miss Grace say *pau,* Mr. Stanton."

Millay started to argue, but when Opaka tightened his grip, the handsome features went lax and he subsided. He ran his tongue over dry lips, his gaze lowering, and allowed the *luna* to prod him from the room.

Grace Millay said, "We'll go out on the lanai, Mr. Quincannon. It's cooler there." And when they were outside in the shade of the monkeypod, "You must excuse my brother. He is . . . high-strung and inclined to be belligerent when he drinks too much."

Weak and easily manipulated were more apt descriptions of Stanton Millay. All fuss and feathers, with very little sand; anyone who showed him strength, man or woman, could back him down. Prime prey for the likes of Vereen and Nagle. It was little wonder, Quincannon thought, that Millay chose to leave the ranch for long periods whenever he could. Only in the vice dens of Nuuanu Avenue, Chinatown, and the Barbary Coast would he be able to convince himself and others of his manhood.

He asked, "Does he always drink so heavily during the day?"

"No. At least, not here on the ranch."

"Why now, then?"

"I have no idea, unless it has something to do with the man you're looking for. He hasn't drawn a sober breath since he returned on Monday."

"Returned alone?"

"Alone, yes. What sort of criminal is this man Vereen?"

"The opportunistic sort," Quincannon told her. "He and his partner suit their chicanery to the person or persons they're aiming to fleece. Their specialty is confidence games involving stocks and bonds."

"That doesn't apply to Stanton. He has neither, nor any interest in such matters. Nor have I."

"It isn't clear yet what kind of swindle they tailored to your brother. Something to do with a cloak or clock, perhaps. Does that suggest anything to you?"

She shook her head. "*Were* they able to fleece him?"

"I can't say yet. He claims he had no business dealings with them."

"But you think otherwise."

"I have good reason to," Quincannon said. "You seem to have a strong influence with him, Miss Millay. Can you convince him to be candid with you?"

"Not if he's done something illegal or immoral and a substantial amount of money is involved. The amount would be substantial, I suppose?"

"Yes. Vereen and his partner would not have traveled all the way to Hawaii otherwise."

"Isn't it possible my brother was not their . . . target? That they had another, someone who resides in Hilo?"

"Anything is possible," Quincannon admitted. "But from all indications your brother was their mark. If they did manage to bilk him, any verifiable amount of money or goods I recover will be returned, of course."

"Of course." Her smile was thin and skeptical. She was a handsome

woman, as Abner Bannister had said, but in a severe way. A woman
hardened by the land and by her responsibilities, cynical and tenacious, who would do whatever she felt necessary to protect her own.
"Tell me, why did you mention an *auohe* on the coast nearby?"

He decided to be straightforward with her. "The word was written on a map of the island Vereen's partner had in his possession."

"Just the word? No specific place?"

"No."

"I suppose it could refer to the ruins of an old *heiau,* but I can't
imagine why. You know what a *heiau* is?"

"I do. As a matter of fact I stopped for a look at those ruins before
I came here."

"Then you know there is nothing there that would interest a pair
of crooks," Grace Millay said. "Do you believe that Vereen is not and
never has been here at the ranch?"

Quincannon was not convinced, but he said, "I have no choice
but to take your word for it."

"You're welcome to search the house and the ranch buildings."

"That won't be necessary." The invitation alone convinced him
the effort would be futile.

"Well, then. If you're satisfied Vereen is not here, then my brother
must have been telling the truth about last seeing him in Hilo."

"So it would seem."

"You'll be going there, then?"

"Hilo, yes," he lied. "As soon as possible."

"That would have to be tomorrow. As late as it is, you may as
well spend the night here—we have guest quarters out back. With an
early start you'll reach Kailua in time to catch the afternoon steamer."

Quincannon had no intention of going to either Kailua or Hilo
on the morrow. Lonesome Jack Vereen had no more departed the
inter-island steamer in Hilo than he himself had; the grifter must
have come here with Stanton Millay. Why had Millay—and perhaps
his sister—lied about it? And where was Vereen now? On his way

back to Honolulu, his business with Millay quickly completed? It was possible, but Quincannon had the feeling that that was not the answer. The answer, he was convinced, lay either here on the ranch or close by.

An overnight stay suited him, therefore. He was tired, the prospect of a night camped out in the volcanic wasteland held no appeal, and a morning departure better fitted the initial plan of action he had devised. He accepted Grace Millay's invitation.

17

"I hate this place," Philip Oakes said as he and Sabina approached the Pettibone home along the front drive. "From the minute I first laid eyes on it I hated it."

"Why?" she asked.

"Look at it. It doesn't belong here. It's not a Hawaiian house, it's a San Francisco house. An exact replica of the one my uncle lived in with my aunt before she died."

"Is that why he had it built, as a monument to her memory?"

Oakes emitted a sound halfway between a laugh and a snort. "My uncle didn't have a sentimental bone in his body. Not a sentimental bone. He never loved my aunt, he tolerated her for the same reason he tolerated me—family loyalty. What he loved, the only thing he loved besides making money, was the house he owned in the Western Addition. He hated having to sell it."

"Then why did he? Why did he leave San Francisco and move here after your aunt died?"

"He had no choice, his business partners forced him into it. Expansion of trade with the Pacific and Far East markets meant bigger profits with the base of operations here. He couldn't bring the Western Addition house with him, so he had this one built, an exact copy. The furniture . . . he even had that shipped over with the rest of his belongings. A replica inside and out. Inside and out. It—" Abruptly

Oakes broke off, gave his head a sharp shake. "I shouldn't be talking to you like this."

"I won't repeat anything you've said."

"All right, then. Never mind. It doesn't matter how I feel about the house. I won't be living in this monstrosity much longer, now that he's dead. No, not much longer."

It was not the house he hated, Sabina thought as they neared the front entrance, it was his uncle. The enmity must stem from reliance on Gordon Pettibone for his livelihood, and having to share space not only with him but with the woman with whom he was apparently cohabiting. That was why Philip Oakes drank to excess, perhaps was even a contributing factor in his amorous pursuits. His uncle's sudden demise had not completely freed him of the yoke; only financial independence would accomplish that, thus his desperate desire for the insurance money.

Immediately upon entering the house, even though she had been prepared, Sabina had the eerie sensation of having stepped out of Waikiki and into a stateside manse. The wide foyer was hung with gold-framed mirrors; the broad curving staircase had ornate newel posts and carpeted risers. Through an archway she could see into a parlor burdened by heavy, waxed mahogany furniture and stodgy paintings in baroque frames. There was nothing anywhere even remotely Hawaiian.

The Chinese houseman, Cheng, appeared from inside the parlor. He was short, slightly stooped, stoic; he showed no surprise at seeing Sabina, acknowledging her presence with nothing more than a slight bow. Oakes did not bother to introduce them.

"We'll be in the study, Cheng," he said. Then, "Miss Thurmond . . . where is she?"

"She resting in her room."

"Good. Then she won't bother us."

He led Sabina down a central hallway off which opened other archways that provided glimpses of a sitting room and dining room.

At a short cross-hallway he turned right and halted at a set of double oak doors. There was a six-inch gap between the two halves. A
twisted piece of metal that was part of a bolt lock was visible in the
opening. When Oakes drew one of the halves open, Sabina noted
that a brass key still jutted askew from the keyhole inside.

"How was the door lock forced?" she asked.

"With a poker. A poker from the parlor fireplace."

"Were you the first to arrive in response to the pistol shot?"

"No, Cheng was. Then me."

"And Miss Thurmond?"

"Just after I forced the lock."

Oakes went first into the darkened study, turned a wall switch to
illuminate a heavy brass chandelier. The large room had the austere
atmosphere of a museum display. Neatly filled bookshelves covered
one wall; more colorless paintings adorned a second; damask drap-
ery covered the rear wall. A brick-and-mortar fireplace occupied the
fourth wall, its mantelpiece bare, nothing on the clean-swept hearth-
stones other than a set of brass fire tools and a small stack of cord-
wood. Two overstuffed leather armchairs, two ornate floor lamps, a
smoking stand, and a long writing table flanked by a pair of straight-
backed chairs comprised the furnishings.

The floor was carpeted here, too, the nap a dark tan color on
which crusted bloodstains were still visible despite an effort having
been made to remove them by scrubbing. Sabina made out a dark
splotch near one of the armchairs, faint streaks over a distance of
some three feet, and a smaller splotch five feet from the fireplace—all
of which indicated that Gordon Pettibone had crawled away from
the spot where he was mortally wounded. Not toward the door, however. Why not?

She asked Oakes, "Exactly where was your uncle lying when you
broke in?"

"There." He pointed to the second splotch.

"Facedown or on his back?"

"Facedown."

"And the pistol?"

"A short distance away."

"How short a distance? Inches, a foot or more?"

"About a foot. About twelve inches. Captain Jacobsen thinks that when my uncle fired the shot into his chest, the recoil knocked the pistol out of his hand and it bounced away that far. Doesn't seem likely to me. Does it seem likely to you?"

No, it didn't. The weapon had lain some four feet from the evident firing point, a possible but unlikely distance for it to have gone as a result of recoil. It was also possible that Pettibone had been crawling toward the firearm, perhaps to shoot himself a second time, a *coup de grâce*, but that, too, seemed problematical.

Oakes said, "Much more likely he flung the pistol away after it went off accidentally. Eh? Eh?"

More likely, yes. But only by a small margin.

"Was Mr. Pettibone in the habit of coming in here in the middle of the night?" Sabina asked.

"No. Not as far as I know."

"Why do you think he did so at three A.M., armed with his pistol?"

"Not to kill himself," Oakes said. "No, not to kill himself."

"Why, then? He had to have some reason."

"I don't know. Maybe he was awakened by a noise of some sort—he was a light sleeper—and came down to investigate."

"There haven't been any burglaries or attempted burglaries in the neighborhood, have there?"

"No. But he didn't trust the natives. Didn't like Hawaiians." A frown pleated Oakes's brow. "It doesn't matter why he came here when he did. All that matters is that he accidentally shot himself."

Sabina let that pass, too, without comment. "Did you hear noises prior to the gunshot?" she asked.

"No. No noises."

"Your room is where, Mr. Oakes?"

"Second on the north side, front."

"Your uncle's?"

"Head of the stairs."

"And Miss Thurmond's?"

"Next to his on the south side." Oakes's mouth pinched in at the corners. "With a connecting door," he added.

"Was the library door always kept locked at night?"

"The door and both windows but not only at night. Whenever he wasn't here."

"Miss Thurmond wasn't allowed in here by herself?"

"No. He didn't trust her. Didn't trust anybody."

"So she doesn't have a door key?"

"No, and neither do I or Cheng. He kept his key with him at all times, never let it out of his sight."

Sabina looked again at the stains on the carpet. "Your uncle's dying words—how did he say them? All three together, or with a pause or pauses between them?"

"Are we back to that again? Back to that again? I don't see what difference it makes."

"Please answer the question, Mr. Oakes."

"Let me think. . . ." Then, "With a pause between the last two."

"'Pick up . . . sticks.'"

"Yes."

"Was he lying still when he spoke?"

"Lifted his arm as if he were attempting to rise. In the next second he was gone. Dead as a doornail."

Sabina crossed to the rear wall and opened the drapes. The windows were both casements with double-halved panes fitted into brass frames. A storm shutter covered the innermost of the two on the outside; the other, the one through which she'd briefly looked yesterday morning, had none.

"Why is only the one window shuttered?" she asked Oakes.

"Both were, but the shutter on that one was damaged in Saturday night's storm. Cheng took it down."

"Are the windows always kept shuttered?"

"No. Only during *kona* weather."

Sabina peered at the frames in the shutter-free window. They fit tightly together and were secured by a bolt that turned by means of a small brass knob centered between French-type handles. She unfastened the bolt, an act that required two turns of the knob.

"Are you sure this window was secure when the shooting took place?" she asked.

"I checked it myself. So did Miss Thurmond. Locked tight. Both of them. Locked tight." Oakes's voice was edged with impatience now. "I don't see the need for all these questions. Captain Jacobsen didn't ask half as many."

"I believe in being thorough."

"Do they help prove the shooting was accidental? Do they? I don't see how."

Sabina had become as annoyed with him as he was with her. "You asked for my professional assistance, Mr. Oakes. Kindly allow me to investigate as I deem necessary."

"All right. All right. What else do you want to know?"

"Nothing more at the moment. Now, if you don't mind, I would prefer to continue in here alone."

"You want me to leave?"

"If you don't mind," she repeated.

He did mind, judging from his expression, but he made no protest. He said, "Very well, I'll wait for you in the parlor," and took his leave.

Sabina turned back to the window. The two halves opened outward, letting in the overheated breeze. She examined the frames top and bottom, then the sill. It was less than three feet above the ground outside.

There was a faint mark on the sill's outer portion—a tiny scrape in the wood, she discerned upon closer inspection, neither deep nor long but fairly fresh. There were no other marks on the window casing. But when she felt along the top corner of the left-hand frame, her fingertip was lightly pricked by something caught there.

Carefully she pinched it off. It was a sliver of soft, blackened wood. When she rubbed it between thumb and forefinger, it left a thin smear. She sniffed the smear, then the splinter; both had a faint brackish odor.

She went to the writing table. The top left-hand drawer contained bond paper, some plain and some with a Great Orient Import-Export Company letterhead, plain and printed envelopes, handwriting tools. Sabina slipped the splinter into one of the plain envelopes, which she then folded and tucked into her skirt pocket.

In the top right-hand drawer were two accordion files, one filled with a jumble of notes written in a spidery backhand, the other with a sheaf of manuscript pages penned by a different, precise hand that was likely Miss Thurmond's. Sabina flipped through the first few pages. This was the book Gordon Pettibone had been writing, a ponderous tome with a ponderous title: *A Comprehensive History of China's Five Dynasties and Ten Kingdoms*.

Nothing in any of the other drawers captured her attention. She moved on to the shelves of books on the wall behind the table. Most were old and bound in brown and black leather, a few others in buckram. Judging by their titles, all were volumes of Far East and East Asian history, the preponderance of them concerning ancient China. All, that was, except for one tucked into a corner on an upper shelf. That one, also leather-bound, had the words HOLY BIBLE stamped in gold leaf on its backstrip.

On impulse, Sabina took it down. It, too, was old and seemed to have been well read. By Pettibone's late wife, evidently, for the flyleaf bore her signature. Tucked inside was a two-by-two-inch white index card of the sort she and John used to file addresses at Carpenter and Quincannon, Professional Detective Services. It had been in the

Bible for some time, a fact attested to by a yellowish tinge to the paper and the faded ink of the single line written on one side.

RL462618359.

The penmanship was not that of the late Mrs. Pettibone, but rather the same as that on the notes in the accordion file—Gordon Pettibone's. What did the two letters and line of numbers signify? Some sort of reference to passages of Scripture? No, that was unlikely. And nothing had been written in the Bible itself.

She decided against pocketing the index card. Instead she returned to the writing table, and with pen and ink from the drawer, copied the two letters and line of numbers onto the envelope containing the splinter.

After replacing the card and reshelving the Bible, she opened three of the Oriental history books at random. Each also contained an index card, these relatively new, on which were noted dates of purchase, prices paid, estimated worth, research references to similar volumes. The handwriting was the same as on the manuscript pages: Miss Thurmond and her cataloguing duties.

Sabina looked around the rest of the study. The fireplace, in this tropical climate, was ornamental rather than functional. There was nothing of interest on or under the armchair cushions, or under the armchairs themselves, or anywhere else in the room.

The shutter-free window drew her again. Its two halves were still open; she widened the gap and leaned out to look at the ground beneath. The stubbly grass had been cleared of most of the debris from Saturday night's storm, but it was still littered with leaves and twigs. Needle in a haystack, she thought. Then again, perhaps not.

She closed and re-bolted the window frames, drew the drapes, and went in search of the way to the side porch.

18

SABINA

The side porch opened off of the kitchen. Cheng showed her the way after she encountered him in the central hallway. She took the opportunity to ask that he tell Miss Thurmond she wished to speak with her and to please wait with Mr. Oakes in the parlor. The houseman, used to being given orders and to obeying them unquestioningly, went to do as she requested.

Outside, Sabina went around to the rear of the house. Starting in close to the wall, she walked slowly back and forth for a distance of several feet on either side of the shutter-free window, her body bent forward and her eyes searching the ground. When she failed to find what she sought, she moved outward by two paces and repeated the process. She had to do this five times before her efforts were rewarded.

The first object she spied and quickly picked up was an irregular chunk of light-colored wood the size of a cookie, wafer-thin along one edge, tapering gradually to a thicker, rounded outer edge. The thin portion was scraped in two places, top and bottom. She slipped the piece into her skirt pocket and continued her search.

It did not take her long to find the second chunk of wood, for it was black and of a similar shape and somewhat larger size. One of its edges, too, was thin and flattish, the surface on one side scraped and marred by a tiny gouge the size of the splinter. This piece joined the other in her pocket.

She returned to the side porch and reentered the house. Before going to the parlor, she took a few moments to compose herself. Her exertions in the fiery glare of the sun had made her feel a trifle light-headed. Prickly oozings of perspiration glazed her face and trickled on the back of her neck; her blouse felt as if it were pasted to the skin between her shoulder blades. She loosened the garment, wiped away as much of the perspiration as she could with her handkerchief. Lord, how good a cold shower would feel just now!

Earlene Thurmond was waiting in the parlor with Philip Oakes, the two of them sitting stiff-backed some distance apart and ignoring each other. Both stood when Sabina entered. The young blond woman was indeed Junoesque, broad-hipped and abundantly endowed above the waist. Her eyes were a light gray, her mouth a somewhat pinched cupid's bow. It was impossible to tell what she was thinking as she faced Sabina; her round countenance was as unreadable as a closed book.

Oakes had a glass in one hand; the amber color identified its contents as whiskey undiluted by either water or soda. He had not had enough of it to visibly affect him. His gaze was both expectant and impatient, as were his words when he spoke.

"What took you so long? Did you find out anything?"

"I'm not sure."

"Not sure? What do you mean, not sure?"

"Just what I said." Sabina gave her attention to Miss Thurmond, introduced herself.

"Yes, Mr. Oakes told me your name and why you're here." The woman was attractive only until she opened her cupid's-bow mouth; her voice had a thin, reedy quality that befitted a less statuesque woman. "I don't know what I can tell you that you don't already know."

"Perhaps nothing. Do you mind answering a few questions?"

"Not at all."

"Have you an opinion as to how Mr. Pettibone died?"

"It may have been an accident, as Mr. Oakes believes, or it may have been suicide. The police think it was the latter."

"They're wrong," Oakes said. "Wrong!"

Sabina said, "One or the other, then. You don't suppose it could possibly have been foul play."

Miss Thurmond arched one of her pale eyebrows. "Foul play? Of course not. The door and windows were bolted on the inside. Mr. Oakes and I made sure of that."

"Which of you first checked the windows?"

"I don't recall. Does it matter?"

"I'm just curious. Could it have been you?"

"I believe it was Mr. Oakes."

"No, it wasn't," he said. "No, it wasn't. I remember now . . . she told me the windows were locked when I came back from talking to you outside. Then I went over to have a look for myself. But I still don't see that it matters."

"Were they always kept closed and bolted during the day?" Sabina asked Miss Thurmond.

"Almost always, yes. With the drapes drawn over them. Mr. Pettibone didn't care for the view."

"The drapes were open on the night he died, weren't they?"

"Yes, they were. He must have opened them for some reason. They were drawn when he and I left the study earlier that evening."

"Did he check to see that the windows were bolted before you left?"

"Yes. Usually he did." The eyebrow arched again, interrogatively. "I don't understand what the windows have to do with what happened."

"Neither do I," Oakes said. "He was careless with the pistol, fired it accidentally—that is what happened."

Sabina asked the secretary, "Do you have any idea why he went into the study armed with the pistol?"

"No. Unless he planned to use it on himself."

The annoying Mr. Oakes interrupted again. "He didn't, I tell you! He didn't!"

"How did Mr. Pettibone seem to you that evening, Miss Thurmond? His state of mind, I mean."

"He was grumpy because the book he was writing wasn't going well. Otherwise, he seemed all right."

"Had he shown any recent signs of despondency?"

"Not that I could tell. He was his usual self around me."

"And what was his usual self?"

It was a few seconds before the woman answered. "Demanding and particular. He wanted everything done a certain way."

"Did you get along well with him?"

"For the most part."

"No friction of any kind?"

"Well, he wasn't exactly generous, but you probably already know that. We never had words about my salary, though. Or about anything else. I know my place."

Oakes emitted a rude snorting sound. Neither Miss Thurmond nor Sabina paid him any mind.

"Then you were satisfied with your position?" Sabina asked.

"Yes, quite satisfied," Miss Thurmond said. "It won't be easy to find another that includes room and board. Certainly not in Honolulu."

"May I ask how you came to be employed by Mr. Pettibone?"

"Employed as his private secretary, you mean? I held previous secretarial positions at Great Orient Import-Export, first in the San Francisco office and then in the branch here when an opportunity for advancement opened. He found my work to be exemplary, and when he offered me this position, naturally I accepted."

"Are you planning to move elsewhere now that he is deceased?"

"As soon as I can make arrangements to return to San Francisco.

There is no reason for me to remain here." She added, "Mr. Oakes certainly doesn't require my services."

"I require none of your services, that's right," he said with emphasis on the noun. "None of them."

She continued to ignore him. He might not have been in the room at all as far as she was concerned. "If you have no more questions, Mrs. Quincannon, there are things that require my attention."

"No more questions. Thank you for your candor."

"Not at all."

When Miss Thurmond was gone, Oakes said pettishly, "I don't like that woman. I've never liked her. She's a tramp. A trollop."

The insult dripped rancor and bitterness. His dislike of Earlene Thurmond, Sabina suspected, was rooted in the rejection of advances made to her before or after she had moved into this house. It must have been a severe blow to his ego to think that she was willing to share his uncle's bed and not his.

"Well, Mrs. Quincannon?" he said then. "Can accidental death be proven or can't it?"

"I'm afraid not."

The sound he emitted this time was one of distress. "But it is possible, isn't it? It has to be."

She was growing very tired of Philip Oakes and his obsessive behavior. She was hot, sticky-damp, still slightly light-headed, and not at all inclined to put up with him any longer. She said, "We have nothing more to discuss just now, Mr. Oakes," and started out of the parlor.

He followed her. "What do you mean, 'just now'? You'll have something to say to me later? What? When?"

Lord, give me strength.

"Later," she repeated firmly. "Now if you don't mind, I'll be leaving. You needn't walk me back to the Pritchards'. Unless you have an objection, I will take the same route across the side lawn as I did last night."

He had no objection, or at least none that he voiced. And he had the sense not to follow her through the kitchen and out the side porch.

She felt better after a wash and a short rest in the guesthouse bedroom. She had just finished changing into fresh clothing when Margaret appeared with an invitation to dinner. Sabina declined, pleading a headache. Margaret, fortunately, had no knowledge of her visit to the Pettibone house, so she did not have to make explanations or fend off questions.

The short rest had cleared her head; she sat on the porch to think over what she'd found at the Pettibone house and what it implied. She had no doubt now that Gordon Pettibone had been the victim of foul play. Nor was there any question in her mind of who had done the deed, or of how the sealed study had been entered before and exited afterward; that was the easily solvable part of the conundrum.

What she did not know yet was the *why* of it—the motive, the choice of place and time. Without that knowledge, or at least a clear idea of what those factors might be, she was reluctant to take her suspicions to the police.

She had the feeling that Gordon Pettibone's dying words were the key to *why*. The meaning of "pick up sticks" continued to elude her, yet she felt that she ought to be able to figure it out. There must be something she was not considering. Something she had been told? Something she had overlooked in the study?

There was a stirring at the back of her mind. Could it have something to do with that index card she'd found in the Bible? She fetched the envelope on which she'd written the letters and numbers from the card, stared at the line until her eyes ached. RL462618359. Incomprehensible. Then she thought: By itself, yes, but perhaps not in conjunction with something else.

If only she could remember what it was that she had been told or had overlooked . . .

19

QUINCANNON

The Millays must have had very few guests, for there were no spare rooms available in the ranch house for that purpose. The only accommodation was a single room located in an outbuilding behind the house that was used mainly for the storage of dry goods. Quincannon was conducted there by the servant girl, Mele, while Grace Millay arranged with Sam Opaka to have the Kona nightingale unharnessed, fed, and quartered for the night.

The partitioned bedroom in the outbuilding was small, almost monastic, its furnishings limited to a bed with a straw-tick mattress, a ladder-back chair, and two rough-hewn puncheon tables. There was no electrical service on this remote section of the Big Island; the Millay ranch buildings were lighted by kerosene lamps of one type or another. The one in here was a small flat-wick lamp, the kind that did not give off much illumination. A hanging lantern would produce a circle of flame of considerably more candlepower, but there was none of this type in the outbuilding. Where one could be found, Quincannon thought, was in the stable.

Sam Opaka brought his carpetbag, handed it over, and departed without a word. Quincannon couldn't tell if the bag had been searched, not that it mattered a whit if it had; it contained nothing of value or pertinence to his investigation. With a basin of water and a bar of lye soap supplied by Mele he scrubbed a layer of volcanic dust off his face, hands, and beard, then changed into fresh clothes for dinner.

The meal was served by lamplight on the lanai. Home-grown beef, rich and tender, which he ate mechanically, without enjoyment. He and Grace Millay were the only diners. Her brother, she explained briefly, was "not feeling well" (an obvious euphemism) and preferred to remain in his room. As they ate, she questioned him briefly about his profession but made no further mention of his pursuit of the two swindlers. The remainder of their somewhat strained conversation was on neutral topics.

After dinner he declined the offer of brandy and returned to the makeshift guest quarters. He stretched out on the bed fully dressed, the Navy Colt beside him and his ears cocked, and forced himself to remain awake and alert for any sign of danger. The vigil was groundless. There was no incident of any kind.

An hour past midnight, he rose and went to the door to reconnoiter. The night was silent, the ranch grounds empty as far as he could see, the sky filled with enough scudding clouds to keep moonlight to a minimum. No lights showed in the main house; a dull lantern gleam in a bunkhouse window was the only light to be seen.

He slipped out, made his stealthy way around past the cattle pens and dairy barn. The stable lay ahead to his right, but as he neared it the door to the bunkhouse opened, shedding a swath of lantern light and then a pair of *paniolos*. The hired wagon, fortunately, had been drawn near the corral fence; Quincannon ducked low into the shadows behind it, just in time to avoid being seen. He crouched there while the two cowboys rolled and smoked cigarettes. They took their confounded time doing so; his sacroiliac had begun to ache by the time they finished and went back inside. Straightening, he swallowed a grumble, stretched the kink out of his spine, and hurried on to the stable.

The doors were shut; carefully, so as not to make any noise, he parted the two halves, eased through, pulled them closed behind him. Horses and the Kona nightingale moved restlessly in their stalls when he scraped a lucifer alight. That one match was all he needed to locate a lantern hanging from a nail near the door.

He took it down, shook it to be certain the reservoir was full. Then, wrapped in shadow again, he drifted back out to the hired wagon and secreted the lantern inside the box beneath the seat.

Quincannon was up and on his way shortly after first light.

The ranch had already stirred to life. *Paniolos* and other hirelings moved in and around the barn, corral, and cattle pens; none of them paid any attention to him. Stanton and Grace Millay were nowhere to be seen; neither was Sam Opaka. Quincannon found the cowhand he had spoken to yesterday, Keole, in the stable and together they brought the Kona nightingale out and harnessed it in the rented buggy's traces.

There was still no sign of the Millays by the time Quincannon drove out of the ranch yard. Just as well. Farewells were unnecessary; they would be as glad to see him gone as he was to leave.

Rolling, dark-veined clouds obscured most of the towering slopes of Mauna Kea. They thickened and seemed to follow him, hiding the rising sun, as the donkey clattered him along the ranch road. Once he saw a lone rider far off among the cattle grazing on an upper valley slope. Otherwise he had the road and the morning to himself.

By the time he neared the ocean the sky was a mass of dark-edged cumulus clouds that obliterated the sun. The muggy *kona* heat was already on the rise; that, the restive cloud cover, and the wind that blew in fitful gusts here and carried the smell of ozone, threatened the arrival of a new storm. The prospect goaded him into venting an epithet that made the donkey's ears twitch. But the threat had yet to be fulfilled when he reached the intersection with the Kailua road. With luck, the downpour would hold off long enough for him to complete the task he had set for himself.

The road was deserted; he saw no one anywhere, heard only the thrum of the wind and the sullen mutter of the whitecapped sea. He drove to the *heiau,* tethered the Kona nightingale to the same stunted tree as the day before, then removed the lantern he had appropriated from beneath the buggy seat. He considered donning the rain slicker that the charitable Kailua liveryman had rolled inside the box, decided against it. Even if the storm broke while he was prowling among the rocks below, he would be better off unencumbered by an extra garment.

He had no trouble finding the ancient trail this time. He made his way down to the ledge above the beach. The offshore wind beat at him, stinging his face with spray from the breaking waves. The blowhole muttered and spouted, but its geysers did not seem to be as high-flung as the ones yesterday.

The broken outer walls of the *heiau* provided some shelter as he moved into the ruins. The first of the openings he'd discovered on his previous visit led him, after a dozen yards, into a cul-de-sac of broken, sharp-edged lava rock. The second wound deeper among the massive stones, twisting so that Quincannon had to light the lantern in order to mark his progress, but it soon narrowed until he was unable to fit his body into the slit. Two more passages proved to be blocked and empty as well.

The fifth, at the far end of the arrangement of flat volcanic slabs, had a tight, half-hidden opening. The entrance to the inner recesses of the *heiau,* he judged, partially concealed by reaching fingers of molten lava from a long-ago volcanic eruption. The space was so narrow that he had to suck in his belly and squeeze through sideways.

After a short distance he was able to walk freely again. This was not a completely natural passage, but one that had been widened and carved through the rock at a sharpening downward angle. Its floor had been worn smooth by water seepage; twice Quincannon slipped on the slick surface and nearly lost his balance. The walls were spotted with some kind of moss that crumbled when he brushed against it. The ceiling lowered as he went, so that he was forced to bow his body and move in an awkward waddle.

He had gone more than fifty rods when the slant lessened and the passage ended in a cave-like opening that led into what must be an ancient lava tube. The seaward end was choked off by a jumbled wall of rock, but the section that curled back inland appeared clear. Here it was cool and dry. The lantern's light glinted off a glass-smooth black floor; off streaks of color in the surrounding rock that must be earth minerals carried along by the lava flows and solidified among them.

After a short distance the tube grew clogged again, apparently with the residue of more recent flows, and at first he thought he'd stumbled into another cul-de-sac. Then, passing around one of the boulders, he encountered a slender continuation of the tube. He had to crawl a short way on hands and knees, muttering to himself, all but nosing the lantern ahead of him like a kid engaged in a peanut-rolling contest, before it widened again.

Here, hanging stalactites and jutting stalagmites obstructed his progress. One of the former gouged his neck in passing and earned itself the same colorful name that had made the Kona nightingale's ears twitch. The tunnel narrowed, curved, rose slightly, then once more widened, this time to merge with another, larger tube.

No sooner had he entered this one than a faint current of warm, fresh air tickled his nostrils.

So. The tube must have another entrance, or at the least an out-side vent, somewhere ahead. He quickened his pace, walking up-right now, holding the lantern high. The floor bore small cracks and the footing was more certain. Ahead, the tube widened into a kind of grotto whose walls were lined with piles of round, smooth stones. They seemed to have been arranged by primitive hands into a pattern—the first indication of human habitation. The fresh-air current was stronger here; he had a briny whiff of the sea.

Around another turning he found the *auohe*.

And something else even more momentous.

This section of the tube was some thirty feet in width, its stalac-titic ceiling pressed low as if spread by great force from above. The floor and the lower parts of the walls were grayish black, streaked here and there with encrustations of green and rusty red. Above and ahead, more recent lava flows had formed an embankment of solid glistening black that rose, with another upslope of the ceiling, into a jagged ledge some fifteen feet above the floor. Now the air was no longer fresh. The pungent odor that assaulted Quincannon's olfac-tory sense was that of mold and rot.

Part of the embankment had been carved into a terrace of shelves. On these lay dozens of full and partial skeletons, some wrapped in decaying tapa cloth, others arranged on powdery mats, one wear-ing an elaborate necklace made of what might have been shark's or whale's teeth fastened with braided hair. Piles of bones and de-tached skulls were heaped together in hewn niches. Interspersed among these grisly remains were artifacts of the sort he had seen in the Millay ranch house—fiber nets, drums covered with some sort of fish or animal skin, rotting feather standards, spears and arrows and daggers, calabashes and gourds and woven baskets.

But it was none of this that held his attention and triggered his wrath, even though the discovery was not completely unexpected. He subscribed to the theory espoused by Mark Twain's Pudd'nhead Wilson: "When angry, count to four; when very angry, swear." And so he blued the dank air with a string of sulfurous oaths the original-ity of which would have made Mr. Clemens himself proud.

For he stood not just in an ancient burial cave, but in a modern one as well. The human remains that lay sprawled at the base of the embankment were a long way yet from being a skeleton. And even at a distance, the upturned face was identifiable in the flickery lantern light.

He had finally caught up with Lonesome Jack Vereen.

A quick inspection revealed two bullet wounds, one in the

upper torso, the other just below the left temple. Crusts of blood surrounded the wounds, splotch-stained the rock floor next to the body. Shot and killed here at least two days ago. There was no offensive odor, as there had been with Nagle's corpse; the cold here had acted as a temporary preservative.

Quincannon yanked at his bad ear, hard enough that it throbbed when he let go—an involuntary gesture of frustration. First Nevada Ned, dead of a morphine overdose the cause of which was likely never to be explained, and now Vereen dead of lead poisoning— both scoundrels sent to Satan before he could get his hands on them. Weeks of chasing the pair in Oakland, San Francisco, San Jose, then across nearly three thousand miles of ocean and over two blasted islands . . . all for naught. By design or accident or divine perversity he had been cheated out of his due as a peerless detective. Unfair. Infuriating. Insufferable. By all that was holy, he would not stand for such a finish!

He drew a deep breath, took a firm grip on his emotions. Then, with the lantern held high, he examined the rest of the cave. There was nothing else of import to be seen, no sign of the personal belongings Vereen had carried away with him from the Hoapili Street bungalow. Satisfied, he set the lantern down and searched the pockets in the dead grifter's once neatly tailored, now torn and soiled clothing. Empty, every one.

Vereen would not have left R. W. Anderson's stock certificates and bearer bonds anywhere in Honolulu, of that Quincannon was certain; he would have carried such valuables on his person. The one who had done him in had them now, along with however much was left of the two thousand dollars in stolen cash. Who else but the man who had not drawn a sober breath since Monday, whose fear and nervous strain were at least partly the result of guilt? Who else but Stanton Millay?

But why? Not for the bonds or certificates, the aggregate worth of which did not amount to enough to entice a wealthy rancher into committing homicide. A fit of rage after discovering that he had been swindled? Possibly, but why do the deed here in the burial cave? Murder could be done and bodies safely made to vanish anywhere in this volcanic wilderness.

Why come to the *heiau* at all, for that matter? Unless . . .

Quincannon swung the light along the shelves for a closer look at the artifacts scattered among the bones. None of them seemed to be of much value to anyone except an archaeologist or a museum curator. If something of value had been secreted here by Polynesian high priests in ancient times, it must have been removed long ago.

He started to turn away from the open crypts. In the sweep of light as he did so, his eye caught movement among the rocks on the high ledge farther down. His reaction was immediate, instinctive.

He had already dropped the lantern and was flinging himself sideways when the rifle flash came.

20

QUINCANNON

The bullet missed him and shattered the lantern, sent it bouncing and crashing across the floor. He landed on his right shoulder and skidded into the opposite wall, the boom of the shot repeated in lustily reverberating echoes all around him. Two seconds later the Navy Colt was in his hand and he was squirming into a pocket of shadow behind Vereen's corpse, the weapon thrust out in front of him.

There was a second shot, the slug missing high and showering him with lava chips and dust. Behind him, the shattered lantern had left a trail of burning kerosene, but the reservoir by now must have been a quarter or less full; the flames were low and before the sniper on the ledge above could trigger a third round, they flickered out. The tube, then, was plunged into blackness as thick as india ink.

Quincannon scrambled backward and sideways toward the middle of the cave. Then, again, he froze in place. The stillness that followed was as absolute as the dark. Now he and whoever had been trying to kill him were on equal footing. If either of them fired, the muzzle flash would betray his position and make him a clear target.

A stalemate, but one that couldn't last. Sooner or later he or the shooter would have to make a move.

How many seconds or minutes crept away Quincannon had no idea. In such darkness you quickly lost track of time. And it was difficult, if not impossible, to gauge the exact source of any sounds—both an advantage and a disadvantage.

Well?

His heightened sense of smell picked up a new scent on the air currents. And then something broke the silence—a distant dripping and thrumming. Ozone. Wind and rain. The *kona* storm had commenced outside. Before the ambush he would have grumbled at the fact. Now he saw it as a potential boon to his chances.

The second entrance to the burial chamber must be somewhere up near the ledge where the shooter was hidden, so the sounds of the storm would be louder in his ears. That would make any noises down here even harder to pinpoint.

In his mind's eye Quincannon could see the shape of the chamber and his relative position. He calculated the distance to the turning behind him. Then he made his move, propelling himself backward and sideways on forearms and knees, deliberately making as much clatter as he could.

As he'd trusted, he drew no fire. He skittered across to the embankment, then backward into the turning. The floor there was not as smooth; sharp edges ripped through his clothing, gouged and sliced into his skin. He permitted himself a small outcry at one of the sharper cuts of pain. When his hands or feet encountered loose rock, he sent them rattling across the floor.

Still no rifle fire.

The confusion of sounds was his ally, and so was the fact that the farther he withdrew along the tube, the more the sounds would diminish in the rifleman's hearing. The shooter would have no way of knowing that his target was heading back the way he'd come.

Once into the turning, Quincannon clawed himself upright and felt his way backward along the wall, still generating random noises. He kept this up until he reached the juncture with the first tube and entered that one. He'd gone far enough by then, he judged, to have passed out of earshot. He stood motionless, waiting, listening to the charged silence.

It might have been five minutes or longer that he stood there. He was a man of steel nerves, but the pitch blackness had begun to have a slightly claustrophobic effect on him. The urge to strike a lucifer alight was strong. He countered it by moving a short distance back into the larger tube, then groping forward along the wall— cautiously, now, with pauses after every step to listen for sounds of pursuit.

The silence remained so acute it was like a pressure against his eardrums.

When he finally arrived at the turning into the burial cave, he stepped out from the wall and took the packet of matches from his pocket. He set himself and flicked one aflame on his thumbnail, then immediately snuffed it and flung himself to the side.

Nothing happened.

No rifle flashes, no echoing reports.

He changed position, struck three additional matches before he was satisfied that his trick had worked. The sniper must have believed that escape had been sought through the ruins, and so had gone down to the *heiau* to set up another ambush there.

With a freshly lighted lucifer held aloft, Quincannon moved ahead to where the ledge jutted above. Two more matches showed him the way up to it, and revealed the opening that the shooter had used to enter the tube.

This passage, like the one in the temple, had been hand-hewn through porous rock and proved to be a much easier and more direct route to and from the burial chamber. It wound and twisted narrowly, climbed, then dipped for fifty yards or so. The currents of air grew stronger, the beat of rain and distant thunder gained volume. Up one last rise, and then he could see a slit of wet, gray daylight ahead.

He approached the aperture cautiously, the Navy cocked and

extended. Outside, he could make out a small flat space surrounded by glistening black rock. He eased his head through the opening. Lines of rain slanted down like thin silver needles, but the full force of the storm had yet to be unleashed; the cloud-roiled sky was the color of a livid purple and black bruise. The hiss and pound of waves lashing the shore was like a low cannonade. All he could see was bare rock.

He stepped out, hunted up a declivity that led out of the flat space, followed it until he reached a point where the roiled ocean came into view. A few seconds after that, there was a loud boom and a spout of water burst upward below and to his left—the blowhole erupting again.

Now he knew where he was. The path down from the road, he judged, should be close by.

This proved to be the case. He located the path, hunkered there to reconnoiter. The ledge and the blowhole were now visible, but there was no sign of the shooter. Mindful of the slick footing, he started down.

He had almost reached the ledge when he spied the shooter, forted up behind a rock with the barrel of his rifle trained on the entrance to the *heiau*. The man's identity came as no surprise—Sam Opaka. Sent to do Stanton Millay's bidding, or possibly his sister's.

Quincannon paused to wipe rain and spray from his eyes before he closed the distance between himself and the *luna*. His foot, when he moved again, dislodged a stone and sent it rattling down. It was a small noise, all but lost in the voice of squall and sea, but somehow Opaka must have heard it. Either that, or the man possessed a sixth sense for danger.

Opaka moved with an almost startling swiftness, in one continuous motion levering himself to his feet and bringing the rifle to bear. He fired before Quincannon did, by a second or two, but his aim was off; the bullet ricocheted harmlessly off rock. Quincannon's shot, even though it, too, was hurried, found Opaka's arm or shoulder and caused him to lose his grip on the rifle. But it did not take him down. He shouted something in a voice even wilder than the storm's, and came rushing forward as Quincannon reached the ledge.

It was not in Quincannon's nature to shoot an unarmed man. Then again, it was not in his nature to curry harm to himself by standing on principle. He triggered a round at the onrushing man, aiming low. To his astonishment, he missed entirely—a rare occurrence that he later blamed on the storm and the poor footing.

He had no chance to fire a third time. Opaka crashed into him and sent them both tumbling across the fissured surface of the ledge.

The blowhole spewed a roaring fountain of water just then, drenching them both in its downpour. They rolled over in a clinch, the *luna* coming up on top as foamy water swirled and tugged around them. But he was one-armed now; the bullet must have shattered bone in the other arm and rendered it useless. Even so, he was bull-strong and fending him off no easy task.

A thump to the side of the head rendered Quincannon briefly cockeyed. It also added fuel to his rage. He swore, bucked, heaved Opaka off him. Blinked his eyes clear. The Navy was still clutched tight in his hand; he cracked the *luna* on the cheek with the barrel, a blow that sent him reeling.

When Opaka stumbled upright he was close to the blowhole. In the tube below, the surf snarled and hissed and let loose another jet of foaming water. The boil of it coming out of the mouth-like opening churned up around the *luna*'s feet, caused him to lose his balance. He toppled over, sliding and splashing in the swirling backflow, clawing at the rock as he was pulled backward.

There was nothing Quincannon could do. An instant later, in a wild churning of arms and legs, Sam Opaka vanished into the blowhole.

21

SABINA

The subconscious mind was a problem-solving marvel. It kept right on functioning independently while the conscious mind was asleep, sorting through memory and supplying elusive answers to troubling questions. When Sabina awakened on Thursday morning, she knew what it was she had overlooked, or rather failed to recognize, in Gordon Pettibone's study, and therefore the probable meaning of his dying words and the significance of RL462618359. Combined, they explained why the shooting had taken place in the study in the dead of night, and part of the motive for the crime.

But she needed to verify her suppositions before she acted on them, which meant another visit to the Pettibone house. She consulted the cameo watch she wore pinned at her bosom when dressed; it was not yet eight o'clock, early enough that Philip Oakes should not have left for Great Orient Import-Export, if in fact that was his intention today.

She dressed hurriedly, pocketed the two pieces of driftwood and the envelope containing the sliver of wood and line of letters and numbers, and left the guesthouse. Once again she took the shortcut across the Pettibone property, went around to the front of the house and rang the bell. She had to ring it twice more before Cheng opened the door.

"It's urgent that I speak to Mr. Oakes," she told him. "Is he here?"

Yes, he was. Apparently he hadn't arisen yet. When she repeated the urgent need to speak with him, Cheng allowed her to enter the foyer and climbed the staircase to deliver the message.

She had to wait several minutes before Philip Oakes appeared, clad in a wine-red robe, his usually slicked-down sandy hair hastily combed. Eye bags and other sleep marks made him look even more dissipated. "What is it, Mrs. Quincannon? What is so urgent?"

"It's imperative that I have another look inside the study."

"Imperative? Imperative? Why?" His expression brightened. "Have you thought of something to prove my uncle's death was accidental?"

Sabina said evasively, "We'll discuss that at a later time. May I have that look?"

"Yes. Of course."

He led her down the hallway to the study door. "Alone again, please," she said then. "I won't be more than a few minutes."

"Very well. As you wish. I'll be in the parlor."

She spent no more than fifteen minutes inside the study. Suppositions verified.

In the parlor she said to Philip Oakes, "Now the police need to be summoned."

"The police? The police?"

"Yes. Captain Jacobsen, if he is available."

". . . Ah! Then you do have proof!"

"I believe I do, but not of an accident. Your uncle, Mr. Oakes, was murdered."

Captain Jacobsen was available, fortunately, and soon arrived in a police van with two uniformed officers, who waited for him outside. He wore the same clothing as the day before, the only difference being that his bow tie today was magenta, but his manner was more brusque than it had been in the Pritchards' living room.

"I must say I am surprised that you involved yourself in this matter, Mrs. Quincannon."

"I did so at Mr. Oakes's request. And not because I expected to reach a conclusion other than yours."

"But you did reach a different conclusion. According to the telephone call from Mr. Oakes, you contend his uncle's death was neither suicide nor accident but a case of homicide."

"With just cause."

"Do you suspect who committed the crime and how it was done?"

"I do, and I believe I can prove it to your satisfaction."

"If so," he said, "I will bow to your superior detective skills." There was no irony in the words. He seemed not at all resentful of the possibility of having made an incorrect diagnosis, or of being proven wrong by a woman. A rare breed of police officer, Captain Emil Jacobsen.

Philip Oakes and Earlene Thurmond were called for and the four of them gathered in the study. Oakes, dressed now in one of his dapper suits, was excited and eager, if still somewhat skeptical; he had tried unsuccessfully to talk Sabina into explaining while they waited. Miss Thurmond had not been told why the police were summoned—she had remained in her room until Captain Jacobsen's arrival—but she had to have some idea. Though her demeanor was as phlegmatic as it had been the previous afternoon, there was tension in her movements, her rigid stance.

"You have the floor, Mrs. Quincannon," the captain said. "Tell us why you believe Gordon Pettibone was murdered."

"Murdered? Is that what this is all about?" Miss Thurmond's exclamation was scornful. "The notion is preposterous. He was alone in here with the door and windows bolted."

"One of the windows was not bolted," Sabina said.

"That isn't so, they both were. I told you yesterday that Mr. Oakes and I both checked them."

Sabina went to the shutter-free window, the others at her heels.

"Checked them how? By turning this bolt knob"—she put her fingers on it—"or simply giving the handles a tug? That was Mr. Pettibone's method of checking the windows in the evenings, wasn't it?"

"I never paid any attention. But I tell you the bolt on that window was in place when I tested it."

"It was not in place when he was shot. The two halves were unbolted then, and had been for some time before and after the shooting."

"That is impossible—"

"No, it isn't. Unbolted, but held tightly shut by another means from outside."

"What means?" Philip Oakes demanded. "What means?"

John, in Sabina's place, would have seized the opportunity to indulge his flair for the dramatic and drawn out the explanation, but she had not been born with a theatrical "ham bone." She believed in being direct and concise. She released the bolt, opened the two halves, and pointed out the mark on the sill. Then she told of the sliver of wood caught atop the one frame, took from her pocket the two wedge-shaped pieces of driftwood, held them up in the palm of her hand.

"The sliver came from this one," she said, indicating the mark in the larger, blackened piece, "when it was inserted at the top joining of the two halves. The other piece was inserted at the bottom joining, and both were hidden from view in here by the width of the frames. Together they provided a tight temporary seal, one that passed the handle-tugging test."

The explanation had the desired impression on Captain Jacobsen. "Where did you find them?" he asked.

"In the grass outside," Sabina said. "Cast away after they were no longer needed."

"And when was that?"

"That I found them? After you left yesterday morning, Captain."

"Why were they used in the first place?"

"To permit surreptitious access in the middle of the night."

"By whom? And for what purpose?"

"By Miss Earlene Thurmond."

The secretary said with feigned outrage, "Poppycock! How dare you accuse me!"

"It couldn't be anyone else but you," Sabina said. "I saw you on the beach Sunday, searching among the driftwood cast up by Saturday night's storm. You picked up something small and dark—this black wedge-shaped piece."

"No. I picked up a shell, not a piece of driftwood."

Sabina ignored the denial. "It was the storm damage to the shutter that gave you the idea, wasn't it? That is why you acted when you did. You spent much of your time in this room each day, surely not every minute in the company of Mr. Pettibone. It was easy enough for you to unbolt the window when left alone that day, then to go outside and wedge these pieces into the frames.

"Late that night you slipped out, removed the wedges, and climbed in here. Mr. Pettibone caught you and locked the door after entering, then opened the drapes to confirm your method of access. In some fashion during the confrontation you managed to gain possession of his pistol and shot him. Afterward you climbed back out through the window, reinserted the driftwood pieces, rushed to the back stairs and up to your room, and threw on a robe to hide the fact that you were fully dressed—a process that took several minutes. That is why you didn't appear until after Mr. Oakes broke down the door."

"You have no proof of any of that."

Captain Jacobsen fixed the woman with a stern eye. "You deny these accusations, Miss Thurmond?"

"Of course I deny them. What possible purpose could I have for such . . . such chicanery?"

Sabina said, "The rifling of Mr. Pettibone's safe."

Oakes, who had been staring at Miss Thurmond with an

admixture of loathing and awe, emitted a bleat of surprise. "What's that? Safe? There is no safe in here."

"Yes there is, a well hidden one. Your uncle must have had it installed when the house was built, long before you and Miss Thurmond came to live here. Either she discovered it by accident, or he made the mistake of revealing its presence for reasons of his own. In any event she knew about it and was desperate for something locked inside."

His eyes roamed the room. "Where the devil *is* this safe?"

"Pick up sticks," Sabina said.

"What? What?"

"The safe's existence and location was what your uncle was trying to convey with his dying words; that is the reason he crawled to where he was found and thrust out his arm—an effort to point, not to rise. He must have spoken as he did, instead of simply naming Miss Thurmond, because whatever she was after in the safe will prove her guilt beyond any doubt. I believe we'll find that it is still there. She hadn't enough time to remove it that night, and while she could have done so sometime during the past two days, with all the activity and the fact that the library door can no longer be locked, it would have been an unnecessarily risky undertaking. Neither you nor Cheng knew of the safe, and she didn't expect that I had discovered it; she could afford to wait until things settled down and she was alone in the house."

Earlene Thurmond had nothing more to say, but if her eyes had had claws, they would have torn Sabina's throat out.

Oakes said to Sabina, "I still don't understand the meaning of 'pick up sticks.'"

"You told me that your uncle spoke those words with a pause between the last two. If he had lived long enough, there would have been a fourth word. 'Pick up . . . sticks . . . wood.'"

"Wood? What wood?"

Sabina went to the fireplace hearth. "The half-dozen sticks of firewood stacked here—stacked loosely, not placed in a container of any kind, and never used because no fire was ever laid on this pristine hearth. I noticed them yesterday but it was not until this morning that I realized that their purpose was not decoration but concealment."

As she had done earlier, Oakes and Captain Jacobsen moved the sticks of firewood to the center of the hearth. Access to the safe was a two-foot-square opening camouflaged by a cover snugly fitted into the surrounding bricks; a layer of matching brick-and-mortar had been skillfully affixed to a thin metal plate, thus rendering it undetectable except on close inspection. A finger hole on one end allowed the cover to be lifted and then removed. The safe imbedded beneath was a small Mosler with a combination dial.

Oakes said, "It can't be opened without the combination."

"I have the combination," Sabina said. "I found it in the same place Miss Thurmond must have, on a card in the Bible shelved with the Oriental history books." She produced the envelope on which she'd copied the line of letters and numbers. "RL462618359. That is the combination, coded by the letters RL for right and left rotations and the numbers run together in order: right to 46, left to 26, right to 18, left to 35, right to 9. I unlocked the safe earlier to make sure that was the correct rotation, then locked it again. I did not feel I had the right to look inside without a witness present."

She handed the envelope to Oakes, who proceeded to rotate the dial accordingly. The safe opened easily to his upward lift. Inside, along with Gordon Pettibone's will and a small amount of cash, was what Earlene Thurmond had been after—an envelope containing documented proof that she had embezzled the sum of two thousand dollars during her employment at the Honolulu branch of the Great Orient Import-Export Company, proof that could have sent her to prison if revealed.

"He was a blackmailer and a sadist!" she cried when confronted with it. Her outrage now was genuine, all pretense at innocence gone. "He forced me to move in here with him, made me work for a pittance, shared my bed at night whenever he felt like it. That's how he caught me Tuesday night—snuck into my room and found me gone. He once told me where the documents were, to torment me because he believed I'd never be able to open the safe. I would have destroyed the evidence if I'd had time to get it, then left here and gone back to San Francisco. But I'm not sorry he caught me, not sorry he was careless with the pistol and it went off when I snatched it out of his hand. I'm glad he's dead. Glad!"

Not one villain but two, Sabina thought as Captain Jacobsen placed Earlene Thurmond under arrest. Or two and a half, counting Philip Oakes. As John was fond of saying, a pox on criminals of every stripe.

22

QUINCANNON

The rainsquall had been brief, having blown itself out by the time Quincannon reached the Millay ranch. Small comfort—he was bedraggled and damp, his hair, beard, and clothing steaming perceptibly in the afternoon heat. And he was still furious, though an effort of will had tamped the fury down to a controlled simmer.

He found Grace Millay in the stable, helping one of the *paniolos* tend to a newborn colt. Her surprise at seeing him might or might not have been genuine. He drew her outside, out of earshot of any of the ranch hands.

She showed little emotion while he gave her a terse account of what he'd found in the *heiau*'s burial chamber and what had transpired afterward, but the news of Sam Opaka's death struck her like a blow. She wavered, then steadied herself against the stable wall with her eyes squeezed shut. It took half a minute for her to regain her equilibrium. When she opened her eyes again, it was as if she had never lost control at all.

"I did not send him after you," she said.

Quincannon reserved judgment as to whether or not she was telling the truth. "If not, then your brother did."

"My brother." She spoke the two words with anger and a measure of disgust. "Yes, Sam would have gone on his orders. He was fiercely loyal to both of us."

"Loyal enough to commit mayhem, evidently."

"I don't believe he was trying to kill you."

"No? Why?"

"Native Hawaiians consider a *heiau,* even the ruins of one, a forbidden place. Sam would never have violated the *kapu* by taking a life in the burial chamber. To enter it and fire his rifle must have cost him a great deal."

"If that's so, then he wasn't the one who shot Vereen."

Grace Millay shook her head, a gesture of agreement. A vein throbbed in her forehead; the cords in her neck stood out in sharp relief. "It couldn't have been Sam."

"Did you know about the murder before now?"

"No. What I told you yesterday is the truth—I never saw the man, never knew he existed until you came."

"But you did know about the chamber."

"Yes. It's the burial place of the high priest who ordered the *heiau* built, and of his family. Stanton and I found it when we were children. I am not proud of this, but after my father died, we brought some of the artifacts up here to the house. You must have noticed them in the parlor."

"Objects of value?"

"Not particularly," she said. "The Polynesians who inhabited this coast were not of the ruling class."

Quincannon believed her now. He said, "All right. Where can I find your brother?"

"He's not here. He and one of the hands rode out shortly after you left to check on the herd."

"When will he be back?"

"I don't know, but it shouldn't be long."

The prospect of a wait, however short, was an added scrape on Quincannon's nerves. Even if Grace Millay were willing to act as a guide, he was not about to demand the use of a horse and go chasing after her brother in unknown territory. His only option was to go with her to the ranch house, where they occupied chairs under the monkeypod tree on the lanai. Neither of them had anything more to say to the other; they sat in brooding silence.

Time seemed to have slowed to a crawl, but it could not have been more than half an hour before hoofbeats in the ranch yard announced the return of Stanton Millay. By the time he and the *paniolo* named Keole dismounted their *lios* at the corral, Quincannon was on his feet and hurrying across the yard, Grace Millay at his heels.

A scowl warped Millay's handsome features when he spied Quincannon. He came striding toward him, stopped a few feet away. His bloodshot eyes and sweating face bore witness to the hangover he was suffering, and to an attempt to cure it by taking more *okolehao* along on his ride.

"What the hell are you doing back here?" he demanded. "I told you yesterday I don't want you on my property. Get off and stay off."

"Not until I'm good and ready."

"*Now*, goddamn it." Millay laid his hand on the butt of the side-arm holstered at his belt.

Quincannon immediately swept the tail of his jacket back, gripped the Navy's handle. "Draw your weapon, Millay," he said, cold and hard, "and I swear you'll regret it."

Short, tense standoff. The *paniolo*, Keole, wanted no part of it; he moved several paces to one side, out of the line of fire. Grace Millay did the opposite. She stepped forward, not quite between Quincannon and her brother, and in one quick movement she jerked the pistol out of his holster and backed off with it.

Millay made no attempt to regain control of the weapon. All he did was yank off the sweat-stained cowboy hat he wore, slap it hard enough against his thigh to raise a thin puff of dust. His eyes avoided Quincannon's now. There would be no further trouble from him.

"We'll go into the house, the three of us," his sister said to him.

"What for? Listen—"

"No, you listen." She made a shooing gesture to Keole. Then, when the *paniolo* was out of earshot, "Sam is dead."

". . . What?"

"You heard me. Sam . . . is . . . dead!"

"Oh, Christ. How—?"

"Not out here. In the house."

Millay followed her there without protest; Quincannon followed him. They went into the large front room containing the array of pagan objects. Grace Millay crossed to the mantelpiece, laid the pistol down next to one of the feathered fetishes displayed there. While she was doing that, Millay turned abruptly and faced Quincannon, his bloodshot eyes flashing.

"You! *You* killed Sam Opaka—"

His sister said, "No, he didn't," and then stepped in close and fetched him an open-handed, roundhouse slap. The blow had the force of a whip crack, staggering him. "They fought and the tide dragged Sam into the blowhole. A terrible way to die."

Quincannon said, "I believed he was trying to kill me. On your orders, Millay."

"No! I didn't tell him to kill you. Only to follow you and scare you off if you . . ."

"If I went into the ruins and found the burial chamber—and what you left there."

That brought a faint moaning sound out of Millay. He sank heavily into the chair he'd occupied the day before, reached for the decanter on the adjacent table. Grace Millay made a move to take it away from him, but he swung away from her and clutched it tight to his chest the way a child clutches a favorite toy. She watched disgustedly as with both hands he poured *okolehao* into a glass, then took a long, shuddery swallow.

Quincannon said to him, "I found Vereen's body in the *heiau*. Why did you kill him?"

"I—"

"Don't waste my time denying it. Why?"

Millay lowered the glass, wiped his free hand across his mouth. His voice, when it came, was low and thick with self-pity. "Self-defense. The bastard gave me no choice. He was angry enough to use his pistol on me when he saw there was no cloak among the artifacts . . ."

"Cloak?"

"Damn nonexistent *'ahu 'ula*."

"You stupid fool!" his sister snapped at him. "What possessed you to claim there was an *'ahu 'ula* in the ruins?"

Millay couldn't look at her. He said nothing.

"A *mahiole*, too, I suppose?"

His chin dipped in a jerky affirmative.

Quincannon asked, "*'Ahu 'ula? Mahiole?*"

"Feathered cloaks and helmets," she said, "made of hundreds of thousands of colored feathers from the *mamo* and other birds tied into woven nettings. Symbols of the highest rank of the *noho ali'i*, the ruling Polynesian chiefs believed to be descended from the gods."

"Valuable?"

"Very. And extremely rare. No such garments were ever in the *heiau* here. They were not made for high priests, only chiefs like Kamehameha for spiritual protection."

Millay took another swallow of *okolehao*, his hand so unsteady that his front teeth clicked against the glass and some of the liquid spilled down over his chin. "I was trying to impress a . . . a woman in San Francisco . . . I didn't see any harm in making the claim so far from home."

"A whore, you mean," Grace Millay said in harsh tones, "and you were drunk at the time."

"All right, yes, a whore and I was drunk. Those two, Varner and Reno or whatever their names, were there and overheard. They struck up an acquaintance . . . claimed to be businessmen, sports . . . asked me questions about the cloak and helmet."

"And you told them more lies."

"I didn't think I'd see them again. But then I . . . I made the mistake of saying I was about to sail for home and they turned up on the steamer."

"With a proposition, no doubt," Quincannon said.

"Yes, but not right away. After we docked they talked me into staying over in Honolulu for a few days, showing them the . . . the nightlife."

Setting him up, Quincannon thought, while pandering to their vices in a new and exotic locale. No wonder they had seized the opportunity to come to Hawaii. A fatally bad choice for both of them, as it turned out. There was a certain fitting irony in that, he supposed, despite the fact that he had had no hand in their downfall.

"So then you sent them to Justo Gomez."

Another jerky nod. "They said they didn't like hotels, that they wanted a private place to stay."

"And Gomez not only supplied them with the Hoapili Street bungalow, but with female company."

". . . I didn't have anything to do with that."

His sister muttered something under her breath.

Quincannon asked, "When did they spring their proposition on you?"

"Last Saturday, at the bungalow."

"What was the game?"

"I'd give them the cloak and helmet, they'd broker them to a rich collector of antiquities they knew about, and we'd split the proceeds. But I think . . . now . . ." A muscle in Millay's cheek flexed and commenced a nervous fluttering. "Just a lie, a damn ruse. All along they were planning to . . ."

"To steal the cloak and helmet," Quincannon finished for him, "and dispose of you once they had them." Like as not true, if such artifacts were as valuable as Grace Millay had indicated. Those two jackals had been entirely capable of cold-blooded murder if enough money were to be had.

"That's right," Millay said, "but I didn't think so then. I thought . . . I don't know what I thought. I tried to tell them I'd made up the story but they wouldn't believe me. They threatened me, threatened Grace . . . I had to keep playing along. What else could I do?"

Quincannon produced the crude map, held it in front of Millay's face. "Who drew this? You?"

"Yes."

"Willingly?"

"No. The fat one, Reno . . . he insisted."

And Vereen had overlooked the map or been unable to find it after Nevada Ncd's demise. "They both intended to take the interisland steamer with you on Sunday?"

"That's what they said."

"Did Vereen tell you why he was alone when he met you at the dock, that his partner was dead?"

"No," Millay said. "I didn't know about Reno until you told me. All he said was that the heat and humidity had laid his partner low."

The kona weather might or might not have been a contributing factor in Nevada Ned's death. Heart failure, accidental morphine overdose, or deliberate act of murder by Vereen . . . there was no way that Quincannon would ever know which it had been. Not that it mattered a great deal, now.

He said, "And on Monday, after an overnight stay in Kailua, you brought Vereen straight to the *heiau*."

"He made me take him there. I kept trying to convince him that I'd made it all up, but he wouldn't listen."

"What happened in the burial cave?"

"He was . . . crazy mad when he saw that the cloak and helmet weren't there. He accused me of taking it to the ranch, wanted to come here. . . . I couldn't let him do that, I was afraid for Grace. . . ."

"Liar," she said.

"He drew his pistol and I . . . I fought him for it and it went off . . ."

"Twice?" Quincannon said.

"What?"

"He was shot twice. You somehow gained possession of the pistol and put two bullets in him, deliberately. That is what actually happened, isn't it."

Millay shook his head, the motion making him wince. "I don't remember. I don't want to remember."

Quincannon let the lie pass unchallenged. "But you do remember emptying his pockets and disposing of his luggage."

"I . . . was afraid to leave anything that might identify him if the body were ever found."

"No, you weren't. You wanted whatever of value he had on him. He had to have been carrying cash, and stock certificates and bearer bonds from the swindle that brought me over here. What did you do with them?"

"Brought them here. I couldn't just throw them into the sea with his carpetbag, could I?"

When neither Quincannon nor his sister answered him, Millay ingested more *okolehao* and then staggered to his feet. They followed him into another room, one which contained a rolltop secretary desk. Millay opened it, handed Quincannon the contents of one of the drawers.

The certificates and bearer bonds were all there; Vereen and Nagle had made no attempt to dispose of any of them, other than the one bond they'd cashed in San Jose, before embarking for Hawaii. But they had spent most of the two thousand dollars they'd filched from R. W. Anderson, or they had if the amount Quincannon counted—three hundred and ninety dollars in greenbacks—was the full sum that Vereen had been carrying. Millay swore it was, but Quincannon was not about to accept his word.

The three of them returned to the front room. He said then to Millay, "You will arrange for a bank draft, payable to John Quincannon, in the amount of one thousand six hundred and ten dollars."

"Why should we do that?" Grace Millay asked.

He told her why.

"And then what? What do you intend to do about the dead man in the burial cave?"

Somewhat mollified now, Quincannon said, "Nothing, as long as the draft is honored at your Honolulu bank. Even though Vereen was shot twice I have no proof to refute the veracity of your brother's claim of self-defense. As for Vereen's remains . . . if the bones of ancient priests have no objection to those of a murdering thief lying among them, I have none either."

Grace Millay said to her brother, her voice cold and bitter, "I'll never forgive you for what you've done. If it weren't for your drunken lies and stupidity, Sam Opaka would still be alive. I wish it had been you who was dragged into the blowhole instead of him."

Millay let out a heavy sighing breath, sank down again into the chair, and cradled his head in his hands.

23

SABINA

The long period of *kona* weather finally ended on Friday. Sabina awoke to a cloudless sky of brilliant blue and a gentle offshore breeze. The temperature, as the day progressed, was a dozen or more degrees cooler. This at last was the Hawaii lauded by Twain and Stevenson—softly scented trade winds, cheerful natives swimming in balmy surf, the ocean placid and of a pleasing apple-green hue. Spirit-lifting, all of it.

She viewed the change as a good omen of things to come. And so it was, for John returned safe and sound late that afternoon. His journey to the Big Island had had positive results, though not quite as he would have preferred them to be. Lonesome Jack Vereen was dead, too—both he and Nevada Ned also victims of the "dying weather," Sabina thought but did not say when told. John, fortunately, was not responsible. His account of how Vereen had died, of the nonexistent feathered cloak conjured up by Stanton Millay that had brought the scheming pair to Hawaii, of his harrowing experience in the ancient temple (the danger to him which he likely minimized to spare her), was related without his usual ebullience at the close of a difficult investigation.

The reason, of course, was disappointment; he had had no hand in the downfall of either man, and thus he felt robbed of the satisfaction of bringing at least one of them to justice after his long and difficult hunt. It nettled his pride, his ego. Understandable, given the somewhat vainglorious man he was, but in Sabina's view, not particularly valid.

"You recovered our client's stock certificates and all but one of the bearer bonds," she said to him. "That is the important thing, my dear—that, and the fact that those two scoundrels will lie, cheat, and steal no more. Mr. Anderson will be very grateful."

"I expect so," John admitted. "But I still wish I had been the one to end Vereen's foul career, if not Nagle's."

"Yes, but think of the difficulties his capture alive would have entailed."

"Difficulties?"

"Transportation of the prisoner to Kailua, to Hilo, to Honolulu, to the police. Explanations, questions, written statements . . . a lengthy, arduous, and disagreeable procedure. This way, you have been saved all of that."

It was plain from his expression that he hadn't considered this. "I suppose you're right. Still . . ."

"I *know* I'm right," she said a touch ruefully. "I spent most of Wednesday and part of yesterday in a similar procedure with the Honolulu police."

"You did?" Surprise made him blink and then fluff his beard. "For what reason?"

"Well, I had a professional adventure of my own while you were gone."

"What sort of adventure?"

"One you wouldn't have minded sharing. The next-door neighbor, Gordon Pettibone, was shot to death in his locked study early Tuesday morning. It appeared at first to be either accident or suicide, but it was neither. He was murdered."

"The devil you say. But how did you become involved?"

She explained in detail—how she first learned of Pettibone's death, how her aid had been enlisted by Philip Oakes, and how she had deduced the explanations for the crime's complexities.

John was genuinely impressed. "A stellar piece of detective work, my love," he said. "I couldn't have done better myself."

"Praise of the highest order," she said with only a hint of irony.

"That lecherous fop Oakes must have been thrilled. Death by homicide doesn't invalidate his uncle's insurance policy. He'll collect the full twenty thousand dollars."

"Thrilled for that reason, and because his uncle's death released him from bondage and Miss Thurmond's arrest removed her from his life as well. The property is his alone now, at least until the will is probated."

"He has access to enough money to pay our fee, I trust? We won't have to wait until he collects the insurance?"

"Well, actually, John, I didn't charge him a fee."

"You didn't? Why the deuce not? He didn't expect you to investigate gratis, did he?"

"No, he offered to pay our usual rate, but I'm afraid I declined."

"Declined?" He gave her a half-pained, half-reproving look. "Why? Were you giddy from the heat?"

"Perhaps. But since I have no professional standing here, it seemed a reasonable thing to do at the time."

"It's not a reasonable thing to do at *any* time, professional standing or not," John said. "Well, we'll soon rectify the error. You will present Philip Oakes with a bill for services rendered and I will make sure he pays it before we leave Honolulu."

Sabina didn't argue. She was not always in accord with John's obsession with the almighty dollar, but in this particular case she was. That lecherous fop Philip Oakes blessed well *ought* to pay and pay handsomely for her services!

If he had had his way, they would have booked passage on the next available steamship bound for San Francisco. A desire to report to R. W. Anderson and return the stock certificates and bearer bonds was one reason, the bad taste left by the deaths of Vereen and Nagle and his misadventures on the Big Island another. But the primary reason was that he missed the city and its familiar haunts, and Carpenter and Quincannon, Professional Detective Services. The old bromide that absence makes the heart grow fonder was never truer than when your home and business were seven days and almost three thousand miles distant.

Sabina, however, was less eager to leave. Now that the weather had improved, the attractions of Waikiki and Honolulu, combined with the well-meaning blandishments of Margaret Pritchard, had her yearning to prolong the vacation aspects of their visit. The matter was settled at dinner with the Pritchards that evening, when Lyman offered to arrange for their first-class passage on an Oceanic steamer from Australia scheduled to depart Honolulu on Tuesday. The prospect of three more days on the island put a sparkle in Sabina's eyes that Quincannon could not bring himself to dim. Only an unfeeling dolt—he was many things, but that was not one of them—would deny his bride, his partner, and his best friend a simple pleasure. A well-earned one, too, for Philip Oakes had paid the bill she gave him promptly and without complaint.

As it turned out, the delay in their departure was not without benefit for Quincannon, too. On Saturday, Lyman and Margaret took them on a picnic in lush Manoa Valley, and on Sunday to a native *luau* replete with traditional Polynesian music and dancing, and succulent roast pig. He found these outings almost as enjoyable as how he and Sabina spent their last day on Waikiki, which was to do nothing more than swim in the ocean and lie indolently in the shade of coconut palms.

Both Lyman and Margaret accompanied them to the harbor on Tuesday afternoon. Sabina and Margaret had become staunch friends, a bond strengthened by Sabina's sterling efforts in the Pettibone matter; they promised to write regularly and to arrange a get-together when the Pritchards made their annual trip to San Francisco the following year, and Margaret issued an open invitation for another island visit. The get-together, if not the invitation, suited Quincannon. His small coterie of social acquaintances did not normally include corporation executives, but Lyman was more congenial by far than any he'd dealt with in California.

When the Oceanic steamer sailed out of Honolulu Harbor, he stood with Sabina at the rail for his last glimpse of Hawaii's tropical lushness. Now that he was departing, he had to admit that his feelings toward the Islands had mellowed. They had a certain amount of allure, to be sure. Although another visit was unlikely given the demands of their profession, he supposed he might not be averse to it someday to please Sabina.

The mellowness lasted until the steamer was two days from the Golden Gate. That was when a sudden storm as fierce as those on the westbound crossing set the sea a-churn, the ship to pitching and rolling, and Quincannon lurching to their stateroom.

He lay abed, green-gilled and groaning despite Sabina's tender ministrations, and silently vowed that he would shoot himself before he took another ocean voyage. As for paradise, he thought morosely, one man's version was another man's aversion. Travel to such a place was all in the eye—and the stomach—of the beholder.